RF

PICTURE PERFECT

When Alex inherits her grandmother's cottage in St. Ives, she
decides to relocate there to escape
painful memories. She is delighted
to discover that the painting she had
always loved as a child is still there.
But local craftsman Quinn discovers
that the picture on the surface is
hiding another — potentially very
important — painting underneath.
And it would seem that both Alex
and Quinn also need to open up
about what's underneath, in order to
have a chance at happiness . . .

JANET THOMAS

◆

PICTURE PERFECT

Complete and Unabridged

LINFORD
Leicester

First published in Great Britain in 2015

First Linford Edition
published 2016

A catalogue record for this book is available
from the British Library.

ISBN 978–1–4448–2805–4

Published by
F. A. Thorpe (Publishing)
Anstey, Leicestershire

Set by Words & Graphics Ltd.
Anstey, Leicestershire
Printed and bound in Great Britain by
T. J. International Ltd., Padstow, Cornwall

This book is printed on acid-free paper

1

So here I was at last. Back in my childhood haven. The taxi negotiated a narrow, winding street, and deposited me and my luggage outside the familiar green front door.

The tiny granite-fronted cottage was crammed higgledy-piggledy into the row between others like it, the whole lot looking as if they could collapse and tumble down the street at any time. Stone steps led up to the door, grey now from neglect; as was the knocker, a brass lion's head which used to gleam like gold in the sunshine. In my long-ago memory, Grandma's steps always sparkled too, kept white by her meticulous weekly scrubbing.

I turned the key and briskly pulled my luggage over the threshold. I could see the lace curtains next door were twitching already and had no desire at the moment to be drawn into conversation with my neighbour.

Inside, wooden stairs led to the two bedrooms on the upper floor; the downstairs was only one large room which served as kitchen, eating and sitting space. A granite hearth took up most of one wall, and over it hung the picture.

Ah, the picture! A painting which had been my very favourite thing in the whole house. Much of my young life had been spent here, when my mother was gravely ill. I loved this cottage, Grandma and St. Ives far more than my real home.

I had stood in front of this painting as I was doing now, and my younger self took over as I remembered wishing I could walk right into it, like Alice through the looking glass.

A country scene, where a narrow lane led round a corner to a glimpse of the sea in the distance. There was a thatched cottage to one side, its garden full of hollyhocks and roses. Coming up the lane was a man leading a horse, while two little girls in starched pinafores perched on the wall waving to him.

I used to make up stories in my head about the characters, and as I grew older, I asked Grandma several times about it. Where was it? Who painted it? Where did she get it from?

'Oh, I don't know, my handsome.' She raised a flushed face from the oven and pulled out a tray of saffron buns. Dear Grandma. A lump came to my throat as I pictured the familiar figure. I felt that if I turned my head, there she would be, smoothing down her apron, a gentle smile creasing her rosy face. I could smell those buns now.

'It was always in our house when I was a girl.' She shrugged. 'I don't know where 'tis to, nor even if it's a real place at all, or no.'

Well, I was an adult now, the picture was mine, and at that moment I decided I was going to find out anything and everything I could about

3

it. I was in St. Ives, wasn't I? Where every other person was an artist, where all the famous names came to take advantage of the extraordinary light to be found here. There had been an artists' colony here for years. Where better to start asking questions?

I reached up and gently lifted it down. Close to, I could see it had darkened from its years of living above the fireplace, and was greatly in need of cleaning. The frame, too, was very old-fashioned, and far too heavy for the subject. I left it propped against a wall until I had settled in and had time to spare.

Meanwhile, I leaned on the window-sill, my gaze on the sparkling sea, and sighed with contentment. My spirits gave a little lift as I relaxed and put the whole long journey from Paddington behind me. The best part had been the last beautiful sweep around the bay . . . and the worst, my embarrassing moment as I stood up to admire it . . .

* * *

. . . 'Oh, how lovely!' I remembered myself saying. The words were out before I realised I'd been speaking aloud.

The elderly lady opposite, with a blue rinse and a kindly smile, looked up as I spoke. There were not many people in the train, considering it was August month. The carriage was one of the new open ones, like a bus. Further along, a tall, thin young man wearing head-phones was rummaging in a rucksack, and behind me were a couple with two children.

'People say it's the most beautiful train ride in Britain,' she replied and laid her magazine on one side to gaze, like me, out of the window.

We had just left behind the estuary of the river Hayle, where a multitude of birds were finding rich pickings in the silt at low tide. Now the little train was curving around an arc of the most golden sand I'd ever seen, edged by a sea of cornflower blue. In the distance, a lighthouse perched on a small island just off shore.

'I think I'd go along with that.' I smiled, and as I turned back to my companion, my glance met that of the young man and we held eye contact for a second. He had an arresting face, narrow, with a high forehead and large brown eyes. A neat goatee beard and floppy dark hair.

The smile must have still been on my face, however, for he paused and raised one eyebrow before smiling back. I felt myself redden. Oh dear, he thought I was smiling at him! Of course, he hadn't heard our conversation. But there was nothing I could do about it.

'On holiday, are you, dear?' enquired the woman in a broad Cornish accent, who was obviously a local herself.

'Oh, er, no . . . Yes. Well, that is . . . an extended holiday,' I improvised, jerking myself back to my companion and our conversation. There was a limit to what I wanted to tell this person. Pleasant though she seemed, I had the impression she was quite likely to be the village gossip.

And I had no intention of telling her that my beloved grandmother had left me her cottage beside the sea, plus all its contents. I gulped and felt a little frisson of excitement as I saw we were drawing into the station now.

I turned all my attention to gathering my belongings together. I'd put a small bag and my coat on the rack above, and stretched up to retrieve them. Oh, yes, there was the bag, but my coat had slid along and come to rest above the young man's head. I was fumbling for it as the train began to jolt on its approach to the station. And when it suddenly stopped with an enormous jerk, I completely lost my balance and tumbled headfirst into his lap.

'Oh! Oh ... I'm so *sorry!*' I scrambled to my feet, doubly mortified as I felt my face turn scarlet and I met the amused dark eyes turned to mine.

'Not at all.' A wry grin lifted the corners of his mouth as he grasped my arm to steady me. 'Are you all right?'

I nodded and stammered my thanks as he reached for my coat and handed it to me. Then I made for the door and almost fled up the platform and into the nearest taxi.

★   ★   ★

I shrugged myself back to the present as I turned away from the window and the throng of holidaymakers all enjoying the sunshine. Here, people spilled out onto the streets and strolled casually along in the middle of the road. In St. Ives, traffic gave way to pedestrians, not the other way round, and anybody in a hurry soon found they had come to the wrong place.

After settling myself in I slept like a baby all night, lulled by the sound of the surf. Next morning I awoke to the cry of the gulls, the sun pouring in through the bedroom curtains, and a sense of purpose I hadn't felt for a long time.

I found I was ravenous, and soon

demolished a breakfast which I normally had neither time nor appetite for. But I always did eat like a horse down here. Now it was due to the combination of crisp sea air and the lightening of my former tension.

Then I wrapped the painting in brown paper and tucked it under my arm as I set out to walk the familiar streets. I knew exactly where I was going. At the back of an ancient inn called The Sloop was a group of craft studios, specially designed to act as both workplaces and shops where the public could wander in and out, watch the artists at work, and maybe make a purchase as well.

Among others there was a silversmith, a worker in glass, painters, and the person I had come to see.

I crossed the small square and entered the building. It was a fascinating place. I could have wandered around for hours, but I was here for a reason. I passed underneath a stone arch and found the shop I was looking for. The sign over the door read 'Quinn Woodcraft'. In smaller lettering below were the words, 'Picture framing undertaken, also cleaning and restoration work'.

In the window was a display of beautifully crafted wooden animals and birds, together with useful and decorative artefacts. Bowls, spoons, stools; a small coffee table made from a slice of tree trunk, polished to perfection.

I took a step over the threshold. To my sun-dazzled eyes the interior appeared dim, but as I became more used to it I could see a person coming out from an inner room and walking towards me. Tall, thin, dark.

My stomach gave a lurch as I realised where I'd seen him before. How could I ever forget? Here was my embarrassing moment, come back to haunt me. For this was the young man into whose lap I had fallen on the train.

But he showed no sign that he recognised me. His expression was bland, enquiring, polite. I began to breathe normally again.

'Good morning, how can I help you?'
He was clad in a well-worn white apron
with a pocket across the front. Sticking
out of the top were some small tools
and a couple of long, hefty pencils. I
was struck again by how tall he was,
and how lean. His shoulders, however,
were broad and muscular, giving the
impression of great strength, but
contained and understated.

I removed the picture from its
wrappings and enquired about having it
cleaned and reframed. He lifted it with
long, narrow fingers, propped it up on
his bench and took a few steps back.

'Do you know who painted this?' He
arched his brows as he examined it.

I took a step towards him and spread
my hands. 'No, but I've always been
drawn to it, ever since I was a small
child.' I smiled. 'I used to wonder who
the people were, whether they were
related, where the lane led to . . . and
that tantalising view of the sea . . .'

For a moment I was carried away by
my enthusiasm, totally forgetting where

I was. When I realised he had turned his attention from the picture and was looking intently at me instead, I felt myself flushing again. 'I don't know where it was painted either.'

'Really?' Obviously a man of few words, he turned back to the picture.

'That's why I brought it here. I want to find out if I can, now I'm here to stay. It used to belong to my grandmother, you see, but she didn't know anything about it or the artist. She said it had been in her family as long as she could remember . . . '

I could hear myself gabbling in a way I never did as a rule, and consciously made myself stop. What *was* it about this man? Now he was looking at me with that infuriating expression of wry amusement again, saying nothing.

A small silence fell before he looked away and picked up the picture, holding it at arm's length.

'Hmm.' His brows drew together as he studied it. The silence lengthened. The workroom was very quiet, the sounds from the street muted and reduced to a low murmur like that of the sea not far away. Tiny motes of dust circled in the shaft of sunlight coming in the window. I forced myself not to resort to more inane chatter, but the silence was unnerving. I couldn't keep still. I scuffed a foot in a small pile of sawdust and curly wood shavings that released a pungent, resinous scent. When at last he did speak, I jumped like a nervous kitten.

'To me, it has the look of an amateur artist.' He half-turned towards me. 'Can you see what I mean?'

Our eyes met and held for a moment. His were darker than my own tawny ones, almost the colour of black treacle, the deepest brown imaginable, opaque and unfathomable.

I looked blankly back and shook my head, feeling I should have been able to. 'No. I know very little about the finer points of art, although I do dabble a bit myself.'

'Oh.' He put down the painting and

took a step back from it. 'Well, it seems to me that, impressive as it is, for a start the perspective is slightly out. If you look closely at that cottage, it's not quite right . . . it's leaning with the lie of the hill, instead of being quite square. Can you see what I mean?' He peered at it more closely, muttering to himself.

I hooked a lock of my straight brown hair behind one ear and followed his pointing finger. 'Are you an authority on paintings?' I asked, as he sounded so knowledgeable.

'To a certain extent.' He turned his attention back to me. 'I have been on courses and workshops over the years and gained qualifications in restoration work. And through the business I come across such a variety of different styles that I've learned a lot through experience. This area, of course, has always been a magnet for artists, right from way back in the nineteenth century.'

'Yes, I realise that.' Genuinely interested now, I waited for him to go on.

'I expect you know too, there was a well-known group locally, called the Newlyn School, that became world-famous.'

I nodded. 'Oh, yes; I've heard of them, of course, and seen some of their work in galleries, but I don't know a lot about them as people.'

How serious he was. Although he gestured while speaking, the occasional smile crossing his face, I had the impression he was a self-contained, very private kind of person who gave nothing of himself away easily.

I glanced around the studio to avoid that penetrating gaze. Above the workbench hung a selection of tools. I could see chisels, knives, files and others that were unfamiliar to me. A half-hewn tree trunk stood in a corner, the shape of a leaping fish partially visible in it, waiting to be released. Several other raw pieces were stowed beneath the bench.

That was where this man's hidden strength would be needed, of course. Solid tree trunks took some lifting. I jerked back to the moment as I realised he was still speaking.

'St. Ives has always attracted artists by the special quality of its light. And now, of course, we have the Tate gallery here. Have you been there?'

I shook my head. 'Not yet. I haven't been down here for quite some time.' The lump was in my throat again. Not since Grandma was taken into care and died in the nursing home. I swallowed hard. 'I only arrived yesterday.'

His expression softened a little and there was a sudden sparkle in his eyes.

'Ah, yes. On the train.'

2

So, he *did* remember! I felt myself flush and glanced quickly around the room as I fought for something to say to cover my embarrassment.

I gazed at his work and pointed to a group of bird sculptures, so realistic it wouldn't have surprised me if they'd flapped their wings and taken off. There were animals too, regarding me with little bright eyes that followed me round the room.

'What beautiful work you do,' I said, and meant it. 'Do you use driftwood for these wildlife sculptures?'

'Sometimes.' His expression softened as he ran a hand over the smooth flanks of a graceful dolphin. 'This is made from a piece of sea-bleached ash I picked up on the beach over at Porthminster. I use offcuts as well, when trees are being felled, mainly for the stools and tables.'

Now, talking about the subject most dear to him, he was opening up.

'Do you sell many of them?' I touched the feathers of a haughty falcon staring at me from a tall perch.

'It's . . . um . . . a bit patchy.' He ran a hand through his thick hair. 'Usually the summer trade carries me on through the winter, but this year it seems nobody's buying much, I suppose because of the recession. I know my pieces are not cheap — but I have to charge realistic prices for all the hours I spend on them.' He sighed. 'But people are being more careful as to what they spend their money on. No-one's buying the big pieces at all.'

I nodded. 'That's tough, although I can quite understand.'

'Actually to be honest, I'm finding it hard going at the moment. The rent on this place has shot up recently.' He waved an expressive hand around the room. 'And the picture-framing on its own just doesn't bring in that sort of money.'

'I suppose not.' I hardly knew what to say. There was nothing I *could* say; it was too personal a subject to discuss on such short acquaintance. 'Maybe things will pick up before too long.'

He shrugged. 'Maybe they will. Anyway — ' He brightened, perhaps realising he'd said too much. ' — I can always get a 'proper' job if I have to.' He caressed the flank of a leaping dolphin and was speaking dreamily now, as if to himself.

'But I wouldn't really be happy doing anything else. Wood is a wonderful medium to work with, being a living thing itself. The challenge is to release that power and channel it into entirely new life.' He seemed to have forgotten I was there. I wandered over to stroke the tail of a bright-eyed squirrel, subconsciously expecting it to feel soft.

'I'd find it terribly hard to part with something like this,' I remarked, 'after taking such time and trouble over making it.' I smiled. We seemed to be having a normal conversation at last.

He shrugged. 'Can't keep them all. I do hang on to a few special favourites, certainly, but this is a business, you know. I can't afford to be sentimental. Especially not now.' He regarded me steadily. 'So, you paint, you said? Are you any good?'

I was caught completely off-guard by his abruptness. I didn't even realise he'd noticed what I said a few moments ago.

'Oh . . . um . . . ' I stuttered, then recovered myself. 'What kind of a question is that?' I laughed. 'How on earth do you expect me to answer? If I say 'yes' it makes me sound big-headed, and if I say 'no' I'd be undervaluing myself.'

'Of course.' A smile softened his features as he nodded and looked away.

We had turned to discussing styles and prices for my frame when I noticed a couple of middle-aged women hovering in the doorway. Having noted down my order and taken my name, he turned his attention to them.

'Call back in a day or two, and I'll try and have the picture ready for you.' The brusque businessman's expression was back on his face, and he was ushering me out as he crossed the room to speak to the women.

'Thank you, Mr — er — Quinn.' I looked up at his towering figure and remembered the name over the door.

'Just Quinn.' His tone was abrupt and the impenetrable eyes met mine again. I stumbled over the cobbled entrance and left.

* * *

I went back to my very own cottage — my refuge, my haven, my bolt-hole — and closed the door, both on the outside world and on my past life. A fleeting glimpse of Paul's face crossed my mind, but I banished the stab of pain that came with it. I was used to that.

To my surprise, there was a letter lying on the mat. So few people knew I was here that this was astonishing. Holding back my hair with one hand, I bent and picked it up. Opening it, I found a 'Welcome to Your New Home' card, with a message from my best friend Sue inside. Dear Sue — she would have guessed how I was feeling, and sent it so it would greet me as soon as I arrived.

Hi Alex, hope all's well at the seaside. When can I come down to stay? School hols start next week — hint, hint! Love, Sue.

Smiling, I placed the card on the mantelpiece and set about preparing a meal. I would phone Sue tonight and fix it up. She was always good company, and I would take great delight in showing off my new property and introducing her to St. Ives. She'd love it.

In what seemed like another lifetime, we had both been teachers at the same comprehensive. Sue still was, but my circumstances had changed dramatically since then.

* * *

A few days passed in which I cleaned the house, stocked up the fridge and freezer, and actually found time to do a bit of sketching. There was no shortage of inspiration: wonderful views of sea and sky round every corner, wild flowers blowing on the cliff top, and interesting people everywhere. The days seemed longer here, but of course, I wasn't working — Gran's legacy had seen to that, bless her. She'd left me a tidy sum as well as the cottage. And also, I was living on my own again, without any distractions.

But it was time to call in at the studio and see if Quinn — first name or second, I wondered — had made any progress with my painting.

As I went down the cobbled hill toward the seafront, I could see that the tide was right out, and children were playing in and among the stranded fishing boats in the harbour. The brightly-painted craft lay tilted on their sides like great sea creatures. The children's shrill voices vied with the shrieks of herring gulls wheeling above or fighting for discarded fish-heads in the harbour. Together with the raucous music floating out of the amusement arcade, and the chatter and laughter of the passing crowds, it was a lively and colourful scene.

In stark contrast, it was very quiet in the studio complex. Standing back from the harbour, the thick granite walls and sturdy wooden doors filtered out the noise.

There was no-one in the shop as I pushed open the door and entered. Quinn didn't hear me come in as he was right at the back of the room, bending over a piece of wood he was planing. I watched, fascinated, as the rippling shoulder muscles beneath his denim shirt smoothed the wood with steady, regular strokes, and the curly, scented shavings drifted to the floor.

The only sound here was the swish of the plane and the muted cries of the gulls. Little dust motes danced in a ray of sunlight and the scene seemed far removed from the outside world. The man at the bench and the watcher in the shadows . . . we could have been part of an Old Master painting, I thought fancifully

But I couldn't stand there forever, it seemed like spying. So I coughed discreetly and Quinn turned around. A slow smile lifted the corners of his mouth as he brushed his hands down his apron and crossed the room towards me.

'Ah, Miss Rowe.'

'Alex,' I said.

'Right, Alex. Hello. I'm glad you called in. I've got something to show you.' He turned into the inside room and called back over his shoulder.

'Really? I came to see how you're getting on with the cleaning and framing.'

'Ah. I haven't actually started it yet.'

I felt my face fall. Not even started? What sort of a business was this? And hadn't he implied the other day that he was short of work?

He must have noticed my downcast expression, as he hastily reached into a corner and lifted out my picture. 'Well, not exactly. I stopped because I found something that you must see. Look — when I took the glass and the frame off, I discovered this.' There was an air of repressed excitement about him and his eyes were shining as he glanced up at me.

'Oh?' I took a step nearer and peered at the painting. As our shoulders touched, I jumped as if I'd been scorched. But Quinn didn't seem to notice. Standing as close to me as he was, he smelled fragrantly of new-cut wood, freshly-laundered linen, and a faint hint of soap or aftershave. But no, it wouldn't be aftershave, not with a beard. I collected my disjointed thoughts and tried to concentrate.

'As you know, this had a very wide and deep frame.'

'Yes.' I nodded. 'That was one reason

why I wanted it changed. It's too overpowering for the painting, isn't it? And very old-fashioned.'

'Yes. Well, when I stripped it, I was completely taken by surprise.' He paused and our eyes met. 'You'll never guess what I found.'

He took in a deep breath. 'Alex, there's not only one painting here but, I think, two.' He looked at me expectantly for my reaction.

'*Two?*' I felt my eyebrows shoot up in astonishment.

'Yes. The picture of yours is slightly smaller than it seems. The edge of it was hidden by the mount and frame. Look.'

I stared hard as he lifted the cardboard mount and showed me. He was right. 'B-but that means that . . . the one underneath . . . '

' . . . has been over-painted by your artist.'

'Over-painted! Oh, my goodness!' My hand flew to my mouth as I continued to stare, as if by willpower

I could manage to see right through the paint. Like the Alice thing all over again. Then I lifted my head and met Quinn's eyes again. His were solemn now and a slight frown creased his forehead.

'And that's not all. Alex, I deciphered the signature on the original.'

'Signature? I felt a lurch of excitement. 'I didn't see any signature. What . . . who . . . ?'

'That's because I kept my hand over it.' Quinn's voice was level and his expression unreadable.

'But, but, it must be the same artist that painted mine, isn't it? You've found out who it was? Oh, quick, tell me the name!' Giddy with anticipation, I seized his arm and shook it.

Quinn disengaged my hand and I took a step back, realising I was getting carried away. He was still very serious and met my expectant look without a flicker of a smile. Then he dropped his bombshell.

'Alex, the signature on the original is

that of Alfred Nicholson.'

'*Nicholson!*' I gasped. Even I had heard of Sir Alfred Nicholson. He had been one of the brightest stars in the Newlyn School of Painters' universe, and the famous protégé of Stanhope Forbes, its principal. Nicholson had gone on to become a highly-respected member of the Royal Academy and had eventually received a knighthood.

'You must be joking!' Astounded, I felt my mouth dry as I gaped at him.

'I've never been more serious,' Quinn replied. 'The date is there too, look. 1933. I know enough about the man to remember this was the time he radically changed his style.'

He paused and fixed me with a steady stare. 'And Alex, it's always been known that there is one painting missing from that earlier period. It was catalogued, but over the years since, it mysteriously vanished. Do you understand what I'm getting at?'

'You . . . you mean . . . ?' I nibbled my lip as my thoughts whirled.

'That this could be it? Yes. That's exactly what I mean. And if I'm right ... ' This time it was he who seized my arm as his dark gaze bored into me. 'Alex, you could be sitting on a goldmine. It would be priceless.'

The next moment, Quinn withdrew and began to pace up and down, gesturing with his hands as he went. 'Galleries the world over would be fighting each other to get hold of it. You could name your price.'

I gulped as my head reeled and my stomach turned over. I clutched at the corner of the bench to steady myself.

Eventually my brain began to work again. 'But that would mean ... ' I frowned and tried to concentrate. 'Quinn, what would happen to *my* painting?'

'This?' He waved a dismissive hand over it. 'It would have to be cleaned off, of course.'

'And destroyed, you mean?' It came out almost as a wail. 'Oh, no, I'm not having that. Not for all the money in the world.' I glared at him. 'That picture has been part of my life ever since I can remember, and my grand-mother loved it too. I couldn't *bear* to lose it.'

'Oh Alex, for goodness' sake don't be so dramatic! You can't afford to be sentimental over something as impor-tant as this. It's only a daub by an amateur artist, not worth a toss. You *owe* it to the art world to bring the Nicholson out of obscurity.'

Suddenly I saw red. 'I owe the art world *nothing*,' I shouted at him. 'That painting's *mine* and I shall do what I like with it!'

Forcing back the tears of rage that were threatening to choke me, I snatched up the canvas and stuck it under my arm.

I had turned on a heel ready to fling myself out of the studio, when Quinn's voice stopped me in my tracks.

'Alex, wait. I'm sorry.' He laid a hand on my arm to stop me, and I turned back. In the midst of the turmoil however, our eyes suddenly met and held. Startled, I felt an entirely new reaction surge through me, and I was totally unable to move. It only lasted a second, but was so disturbing I felt heat sting my cheeks before I forced myself to step away.

'I was wrong to call your painting a daub; it *is* more than that, I admit. I was only comparing it with the Nicholson, which you must agree, is far more important. Of course — ' Quinn's shoulders slumped and the light went out of his eyes. ' — you were right to point out that it belongs to you, and yours must be the final decision.'

Shaken, both by his climb-down and the disturbing effect it had had on me, I nodded and could reply equally rationally. 'Thank you. Quinn, I need some time to think this over. Will you give me a day or two to do that? Then I'll tell you what I decide.'

'Of course I will.' He leaned over to open the door for me. 'OK then. Bye for the time being, Alex.'

I felt his eyes on my back all the way across the car park and down the street, and had to force myself to appear oblivious.

3

However, I didn't have the time right then to think very deeply about it. Sue was arriving the next evening, and there was a lot to be done, so I wrapped the painting carefully and put it away in a cupboard. Then the time flew by in a flurry of shopping, laundry and cleaning, for I wanted her to see the cottage at its best.

But I couldn't banish the problem entirely. All the time I was doing the mundane chores, it was there at the back of my mind, ticking over and demanding to be aired.

By mid-afternoon everything was done. I had even put a casserole in the slow cooker for our meal later on. With a sigh of satisfaction, I made myself a cup of tea and prepared to relax.

However, just as I was about to sit down, I heard a knock on the door. I frowned. Surely it couldn't be Sue yet, could it? I glanced at the clock. No, no way. Who, then? With a sigh of irritation, I rose to my feet again and went to answer it.

Nothing had prepared me for the sight of Quinn standing on the doorstep. 'Sorry to drop in unannounced,' he said as I gaped at him in astonishment.

He must have noticed my surprise as his tone was apologetic. 'I was just passing. I know you said a few days, but it's been on my mind so much, and as I was so close . . . ' He spread his hands. 'If it's not convenient, of course, I'll go.'

'No, it's all right.' I widened the door. 'Come in. I've just made a pot of tea. Would you like one?'

'Sure, thanks.' His tall frame was filling the tiny room and taking my breath away. I waved a hand towards the sofa. 'Have a seat.' Strangely, I found that my hands were shaking. But he'd startled me by turning up without warning, and it had been a bit of a shock.

'I'm expecting a friend later,' I said as

I poured the tea and we sat together on the sofa in the window embrasure. 'But she won't be here for an hour or so.'

Quinn nodded. 'I found I couldn't concentrate on any work I've got on hand, my head is so full of the Nicholson.' He half-turned towards me. 'I wondered if we *could* just talk about it, Alex. But if you're not ready, then fine; I don't want to push you into any decision you'll regret afterwards.'

I smiled. 'I know the feeling. I can't stop thinking about it either.' His eyes reflected the smile as he lifted his mug and took a sip. 'And I did come up with one thought, actually.'

I felt his interest immediately quicken. 'You did?'

'Mm. I was wondering. If the Nicholson *is* as important as you say . . . '

'Oh, it is, believe me . . . ' Quinn broke in.

' . . . then I suppose it ought to be revealed. And if I could get a really good photograph taken of my picture — by a proper professional, I mean, so I wouldn't have to lose it altogether . . . '

The whole idea was a compromise, but it seemed the only way to please both of us. And, as I admitted to my inner self, for some reason I wanted to please him. Quinn was rapidly becoming someone I liked and respected. There was more to him than met the eye and he intrigued me.

He was on the edge of his seat now, tea forgotten. 'That's a *wonderful* idea, Alex. And I know just the person who could do it. She has a studio not far from mine. Eve Champion. She's really good and is very highly thought of.' He frowned. 'But she doesn't come cheap, mind you.'

'That's all right,' I broke in. 'Not a problem. Good work never comes cheap. You know that yourself.' He gave a nod. 'She certainly sounds a possibility. I'll have to call round and see her work for myself, of course.' I nibbled my thumbnail as the idea became clearer.

'You could even,' Quinn said with sudden enthusiasm, 'commission an artist to paint a copy from the photo, if you felt like it, couldn't you?' He laid a hand on mine and squeezed it as the thought struck him. Something shifted inside me and I swallowed hard. 'I know it wouldn't be the same as your original, but perhaps . . . '

I nodded vigorously. It was easier than speech. Then, as he withdrew the hand — 'Yes', I managed, 'it would be the next best thing.'

Quinn brightened, his eyes sparkling. 'So as soon as you've had the photo taken, you'll let me get on with the work, then?'

'Not quite. You've forgotten something.' I looked steadily back at him and his face fell. 'First of all, I'm determined to find out who painted mine and where it was set. Remember? After that, I promise I'm prepared to give it up.'

He nodded. 'Yes, of course. Have you any idea where to start looking?'

'Not really. At least, not yet.' I felt my face drop. 'It's going to be like searching for a needle in a haystack.'

'Maybe I could help you,' Quinn said quietly. 'If you'd like me to, that is.'

'Would you really?' I felt my expression brighten. 'Oh, yes please. Two heads are always better than one.'

I thought fleetingly that he was being generous in giving up his time; until it dawned on me that, of course, he wanted to get his hands on the painting as soon as he could.

★ ★ ★

I was standing in the doorway, seeing Quinn out, when Sue's familiar little red Fiat drove up and I caught a glimpse of her blonde head emerging as she opened the door. Quinn was just turning the corner of the street by now, and I noticed her head swivel for a second as she looked after him.

'Alex! Wonderful to see you!' Sue jumped out and, as I ran down the steps to meet her, enveloped me in an enormous hug. Sue was bubbly, demonstrative and enormous fun to be with. Only I, knowing her as well as I did, knew it was only a front.

'You too! Good journey?'

'Not bad. Who's the handsome hunk, then?' She hitched up her jeans and smoothed her rumpled pink top.

'Oh, just someone I'm doing a bit of business with,' I improvised.

'Well, lucky you. I could do business with him any time.' Sue grinned and raised her eyebrows. 'Now, where can I leave the car?' She opened the boot and took out her bags, indicating a large people-carrier waiting to get past. 'You said you had a private space, didn't you?'

'Just round the back.' I pointed. 'First turning on the left. It's a tight corner, be careful.'

I picked up a couple of bags and put them on top of the steps, waiting for Sue to park up.

'Come on in,' I said as she returned.

'Just one minute.' She paused on the threshold. 'I must take in that glorious view.' The sun was just going down in a picture-perfect sky of rose and pale lemon, arching over a tranquil sea the colour of turquoise.

'Oh, Alex, what a *fantastic* place! You never told me it was this wonderful. It's a paradise!' Sue looked at me in amazement.

I smiled, trying not to seem smug. 'Well, I did try, but it has to be seen to be believed. Postcards don't really do it justice. We'll go out for a walk later and I'll show you around properly.'

After Sue had settled in, I took her on a guided tour of the town as I'd promised, and we walked back along the harbour in the fading light. When we were home again, she sank down into a basket chair by the window and heaved an enormous sigh.

'Oh Alex, you are so *lucky*. What a heavenly place to live!' I put a mug of coffee beside her and nodded.

'I know. It's fabulous.' I paused and gazed out of the window. 'But you can get lonely, even in paradise,' I murmured almost to myself. Turning back to the room, I sat down opposite her on

41

the chintz-covered sofa.

'Ah.' She gave me a searching look. 'I thought you had something on your mind. So, what *is* the position between you and Paul now?'

'Well,' I swirled my coffee around and looked deeply into it, 'we've been living apart for over two years now, him in his girlfriend's flat and me in our house. He seems content to leave it like this indefinitely. I'm not. I've wanted a clean break for a long time, but I've been telling myself I had nowhere else to go, and very little money of my own. I ended up convincing myself I couldn't do it.' I raised my mug and took a sip.

'But since this place has fallen into my lap, that problem's solved.' I twisted the ring I now wore on my right hand and took a deep breath. 'So, I'm going to file for divorce.'

'Good for you. At last. I wouldn't have waited this long.' Sue snorted. 'A rat like him. The sooner you're completely rid of him, the better.'

'I know that really.' I sighed and

gazed unseeingly across the room. 'I guess I'm such a coward I couldn't face all the upheaval. And the *finality* of it, Sue. You see, I really did love him, once.'

'Well I could never let any man treat me like he's done. I just wouldn't stand for it.' She glowered. 'I don't think I'm ever going in for marriage myself.' A hint of sadness crossed her face, but was gone as quickly as it came. 'After Mick seemed so keen on me, then suddenly changed his mind, and your experience too, I think I'll stay as I am. It's safer.'

She paused and tapped her fingers on the arm of her chair. 'Seriously Alex, if any man treated me like your Paul, expecting me to hold down a demanding job *and* run the whole house as well, we'd fight like cat and dog.'

She leaned back, her hands behind her head, ruffled her curly mop, and drew in a breath. 'Love them and leave them, I say. You can't get hurt that way. There are always plenty more pebbles on the beach.' Her tone was flippant but her eyes were serious. I wondered if she really believed what she said. Sue had a tendency to speak first and think afterwards. I wondered if this might be the cause of this break-up with her latest man.

'Anyway, I'm looking forward to this holiday.' She sat up abruptly. 'Chilling out, pure pleasure, and not a man in sight. Not even thinking about them. How about that?'

'Mm. Suits me just fine,' I replied. 'I've done too much thinking lately.' But even as I spoke, a fleeting memory crossed my mind. Of a dark head, melting brown eyes, and sensitive fingers on polished wood.

'What plans have we got for the week, then; have you made any?' Sue's voice brought me abruptly back to my senses.

'Oh, er . . . ' I sat up and gave her my full attention. 'I thought we might go over to Marazion tomorrow and I'll show you St. Michael's Mount. If you're into the picturesque, that's one place you must see.'

'Oh, yes. I've seen photos of it. It's near Penzance, is that right?'

I nodded. 'But right now, how about going out for a stroll along on the quay? There's a very old pub down there called The Sloop. Do you fancy soaking up a bit of local colour before turning in?'

'Oh, sure.' Sue uncurled herself and rose to her feet. 'I need to walk off your lovely chicken casserole. I've eaten far too much.'

* * *

Next morning, the sun was streaming through the living-room window as I pulled back the curtains. There was no sign of Sue so I called up the stairs, impatient to start the day. This weather was too good to waste.

'Sue, if we're going to Marazion today, we'd better make an early start. Are you up?' There was no answer, so I ran up and knocked on the door of her room.

A muffled grunt was the only reply as I poked my head inside. Then Sue groaned, rolled over and rubbing her eyes, raised her head a fraction from the pillow. She glanced at the clock on the bedside table, then jerked upright in surprise.

'Oh, look at the time! I'd no idea it was that late.' She cupped a hand to her forehead and peered at me bleary-eyed.

'Exactly.' I smiled at her, then frowned. 'What's the matter? Headache?'

'Not really.' Sue shook her head, then winced. 'I didn't get to sleep for ages after we went to bed, that's all.' She yawned widely and thrust her fingers through her tangled hair.

'Oh, I see.' I grinned at her. 'One too many last night, was it?' On the way back we had briefly called in at the pub I'd mentioned.

'No!' She reached for a slipper and aimed it at me. I withdrew smartly and heard it thud against the back of the door.

Ten minutes later she appeared in the kitchen, pink-skinned from the shower, but relatively wide awake.

'Here's a peace offering.' I put a steaming mug of coffee on the breakfast bar in front of her.

'Wonderful!' She took an appreciative sip. 'Thanks Alex. You're a pal.'

'That's me.' I tossed her a slice of bread. 'You're practically leaning on the toaster, so put that in it. Then perhaps we'll get there before lunch after all.'

* * *

'We'll go the direct way today, shall we?' I said as we left St. Ives in Sue's car. 'I thought I would leave showing you the moorland route for when we've got more time.'

'Yes, OK. Fine. Whatever. Just make sure I'm going the right way and not getting us lost.'

I was gazing out of the window as we

47

drove along between green hedges sprinkled with myriad dancing wild-flowers, when she steered the car to the side and pulled in.

'There it is!' she squealed with delight as we jumped out. 'Oh, Alex, isn't it wonderful!'

Below us over a low wall was one of the most stunning views in Cornwall. Appearing to float in a sea of cornflower-blue was a tree-clad rocky island, crowned with a battlemented castle straight out of a fairytale. At its foot was a small harbour with a huddle of cottages standing on the quayside around it.

'Oh, wow! Like I said, I've seen photos of it before, but I always thought they were too good to be true, like St. Ives. I'd no idea it was actually so out of this world.'

'I know. It's awesome.'

'I want to take loads of photos of my own, and I can't wait to see that castle properly. Imagine what the view must be like from up there!'

'Right.' I seized her arm and pulled her back to the car. 'Let's get going. The tide's right out so we can walk across the causeway,' I said as we set off along the beach. 'But they have a ferryboat service too, if you want to cross when it's under water.'

'Oh, that's good. Lovely as it is, I don't want to be stranded over there until the next low tide.' Sue smiled. 'And I can't swim.'

★ ★ ★

That night, we both slept like logs after all the exercise we'd had climbing up the mount, and the following morning Sue was downstairs before me.

'What kept you, sleepyhead?' she joked. 'I've been up for hours — well, at least twenty minutes.' She placed a mug of coffee in front of me. 'And the weather's glorious again, look.' She waved a hand towards the window where shafts of sunlight were already stealing across the floor.

'Ah, thanks. Lovely.' I leaned against the counter as I sipped it and gazed out of the window. 'Sue, I was wondering. Do you want to take yourself off hiking at all while this weather holds?'

Sue was a great one for serious walking, trekking for miles in a day, an occupation that I didn't share. I liked the occasional stroll as much as anybody, but not to that extent.

'Oh, I'd love to, Alex, if you don't mind.' She turned from buttering toast, and her face lit up.

'Of course I don't. You could go today if you want to. I hadn't made any other plans. Go off and get some bird-watching in. I know that's what you like doing.'

For subconsciously I was thinking that here was a chance to go and see what Quinn had in mind when he'd offered to help me in my search. Perhaps he could give me some idea as to where I should start.

4

So, with Sue away for the day, I was free to go and see Quinn. However, as I took the painting out, I noticed some faint marks on the back of the canvas which I hadn't seen before. I paused to peer more closely at it, but in the cottage, with its small windows, the light wasn't very good. Taking it outside didn't do much good, either; the light just wasn't right. I shrugged and resolved to show it to Quinn.

The sun was warm on my back as I made my way to the studio. Early or not, the door was open and I could hear sounds of movement from inside. I hovered in the entrance until I'd made sure he wasn't with a customer. But he was alone.

'Hello, Quinn.'

He looked up from the piece of wood he'd been chiselling.

'Ah, Alex.'

He smiled, straightened up and came towards me. He nodded at the parcel under my arm. 'You've brought the painting then.'

I nodded. 'I wanted to ask if you meant what you said the other day, about helping me find out more about it.'

Quinn indicated the high stool beside the counter. 'Sit down,' he said, perching himself on the corner of the bench and folding his arms.

'And there's something else as well.' I put the picture down on the counter. 'I wanted to show you something I noticed down low on the back of it.' I took off the brown paper and turned it over. 'There are some marks here that I couldn't see properly at home. I thought you might have a magnifying glass.'

'Oh?' Quinn raised his eyebrows, took a step nearer and peered at the canvas.

'Can you see? There's what looks like a faint bit of writing there.' I pointed.

'Oh yes.' As he narrowed his eyes and tilted the canvas towards him our heads were so close they were almost touching. I could even feel the warmth radiating from his skin. When a strand of curly hair brushed my cheek I jumped as if scalded.

'I should think it had been done with chalk, or maybe pencil. It's so faded. But I think it's a name, look, isn't it?'

I gazed at it again as my heart lurched.

'The name of the painter, you mean? Could it be?' My hand was shaking as I stared at the canvas, willing it to speak to me.

'I don't think so.' Quinn slowly shook his head and my heart plummeted again. 'Wait a bit, I do have a magnifying glass somewhere.' He strode off into the deeper recesses of the studio and I heard him opening cupboards and drawers. He was soon back, waving it in satisfaction.

'Now, let's see.' He polished the glass on a corner of his apron. 'No, it's definitely not a signature. But it could be the name of the *place*. There, see?'

He followed the outline with a finger, then stood back and handed me the glass. 'It looks like something-or-other 'Farm'. And a date.'

'Ooh, yes!' I squinted at the faint characters and passed over the glass as he held out a hand for it.

Quinn scrutinised it for a few seconds, saying nothing. Then: 'I think it begins with C,' he murmured to himself. 'C . . . h . . . and what looks like a 'y'. 'Chy' something.'

I looked blankly up at him and held out my hand for the glass.

By now I was beginning to make out the characters too. 'I think it's 'carn',' I replied, screwing up my face. I straightened up and our eyes met.

''Chycarn'?' Quinn shrugged his shoulders and sighed. 'Oh, that's one of the commonest names in Cornwall. It means 'house on the hill'. 'Chy' is 'house' in Cornish; and 'carn', of course, is 'hill'.'

'Not much help, then,' I said bleakly. After the excitement, this was an anticlimax to say the least. 'Chycarn

Farm'. I felt my mouth droop. 'But I suppose at least we know it *is* in Cornwall — somewhere!' I shrugged. 'But, as I said before, it'll be like looking for a needle in a haystack.'

'I was thinking we might be better-off looking for the name of the painter than the place, at first. If we can decipher this date . . . ' Quinn had picked up the glass again and was studying the characters. ' . . . we might be able to narrow the search down a bit.'

I felt a little tingle of warmth at the way he had said 'we', and my jaded spirits lifted a little.

'It looks to me like '1942'. What do you think?' He handed over the magnifying glass once more.

'Yes.' I nodded. 'I'm sure you're right. It *is* 1942. The figures are a bit clearer than the name, aren't they?' I straightened.

He paused for a moment, his brow creased in thought, then nodded. 'Two years after the Nicholson was painted. That's interesting.'

'But Quinn, I haven't the faintest idea where to start.' I sighed and spread my hands. 'I don't really have a thing to go on, do I?'

'How about trying the local art galleries?' He drew in a breath and gazed thoughtfully out of the door. 'Have a word with the curators, show them the picture. They're bound to be fairly knowledgeable.'

'Oh, that's a good idea.' I turned to him with a smile. 'Do you know of any more galleries I could try, apart from the ones just in St. Ives?'

'Well, on a hunch, because of the Nicholson and also because of the period, your best bet would be the Penlee Gallery in Penzance. They've got a wide range of that school on permanent exhibition.'

'Oh, yes, of course. I know of it, but I've never been in there. That's the obvious place to begin. I should have thought of that myself.' Spurred on by renewed hope, my spirits had started to soar again.

'I'll go today,' I added, absently nibbling a fingernail. 'I'll have to look up the times of the buses into Penzance of course. Because Sue's gone off with the car . . . ' I was talking to myself, speaking my thoughts aloud as they came tumbling out, almost forgetting where I was.

'Not necessarily.' Quinn had been very quiet, stroking his beard through-out my monologue, and his voice now brought me back to earth with a bump.

'What?' I stared at him like a fool. 'What did you say?'

'I was just thinking.' He ran a hand through his hair. 'The shop's very quiet today; everybody's on the beach, I think. And I've got nothing on hand that can't wait. Plus, I'm itching to get your picture out of the way so I can work on the Nicholson.'

He gave me one of his slow smiles. 'So, if you like, I could drive you into Penzance and we can go to the gallery together, right away. What do you think?'

What did I think? Part of me was

overjoyed at the prospect of getting on with solving the mystery. And, yes, I'd felt a lurch of pleasure at the idea of spending time in the company of Quinn. It had been a long time since I'd had the company of an attractive man.

So I took a deep breath and raised my head to return the smile.

'That would be fantastic! If you're sure you really can spare the time, Quinn, then thank you very much. I'd love to.'

★ ★ ★

'This building used to be a Victorian family home at one time. It belonged to a wealthy miller called Branwell, who had some connection with the Brontë family, I think.' Quinn waved an expansive hand as we climbed the steps of the imposing house. I could see tended grass and tall trees beyond, with the sea in the background.

'It's a lovely setting. I suppose those were the original grounds.' I glanced over my shoulder as we entered.

'Yes, it's a public park now.' Quinn held the door open for me as I carefully manoeuvred the painting round it. I had to lean backwards to squeeze through the narrow entrance as only one of the pair of double doors was open, which forced me almost into Quinn's arms at its narrowest point. Although we didn't quite touch, my skin prickled and every nerve came alive. I was acutely aware of the heat of his body through the cotton polo top he was wearing. I swiftly focused all my attention on getting the picture inside.

At the reception desk I explained that I wanted to do a little detective work on my picture, asking if there was anyone there who would be able to advise me. The woman behind the counter couldn't have been more interested and helpful. She immediately picked up the intercom and started talking to somebody at the other end. Replacing it, she turned to us with a smile.

'Mr. Rule is free and will be happy to see you. He'll be down shortly. Just take a seat over there if you will.'

I thanked her and turned away. We had no sooner sat down when the clatter of footsteps came echoing down the stairs, and a middle-aged man in a light summer suit came briskly towards us.

'Good morning. I'm Malcolm Rule.' He held out a hand to me, then to Quinn as we murmured our names. 'Come this way, please.' He ushered us forward.

He led the way into a small room off the hall, furnished as an office, with green plants on the windowsill and an arrangement of prints on one wall. He took the painting from me and laid it on the broad expanse of his desk. Before we had come away, Quinn had replaced the mount so that only my own picture was showing. We had no intention of revealing the Nicholson to any strangers.

He seated himself behind the desk and motioned us to a couple of leather armchairs nearby. Removing a pair of glasses from his breast pocket he put them on, lifted the picture, then scrutinised it at arm's length.

'Right, Miss Rowe,' he murmured, 'what made you bring this to us particularly?'

I moistened dry lips, surprised at my nervousness, wondering if he was going to be of any help or not. 'Because Quinn here,' I gave him a fleeting glance, 'told me it resembled the art of the Newlyn School of painters, and that you have the biggest collection of their work in Cornwall. So I hoped someone could help me find out who painted it.'

'And where the place is, if possible. Right, Alex?' Quinn raised his eyebrows as he turned to me.

'Yes, of course. It's all really important to me.'

'Mmm. I see.' Malcolm Rule gave Quinn a long look and nodded. 'So you know something about art, Mr — er — Quinn?'

Quinn nodded. 'I did a study course several years ago,' he replied, 'in London.'

I listened to this with interest, wondering what else was forthcoming, but he did not elaborate, so the other man's gaze returned to the painting, and he raised a hand to brush his blond forelock back from his eyes. A lengthy silence fell as he turned the scene from side to side and peered at every detail. As the time went on I nibbled a thumbnail, tried not to fidget, then glanced at Quinn again. He raised an eyebrow, neither of us apparently daring to interrupt.

'Yes.' As Malcolm Rule spoke at last I automatically jumped and straightened. 'I do see what you mean.' He looked over the top of his spectacles at me. 'This is certainly closely allied to the Newlyn School.'

I leaned forward on the edge of my seat, hanging on his every word.

'But it's not the work of one of the masters. It is very flawed in places.' He looked at me as if he expected some reply.

'Oh?' It came out as a squeak and I

cleared my throat before trying again. 'Then what . . . ?'

'I would suggest that this was painted by an able *student* of one of the greats. It has the look of Stanhope Forbes, or maybe Samuel Birch, about it.' He rose to his feet and crossed the room. 'Now, over here — ' He waved a hand towards the framed prints. ' — are some examples. I'll show you what I mean.'

I joined him with Quinn just behind me, looking over my shoulder.

'As well as being accomplished artists themselves, Stanhope Forbes and his wife Elizabeth ran a school for aspiring students, covering the period when your picture was painted.'

This we knew, but I kept quiet as he turned to me with a smile and spread his hands. 'Purely a shot in the dark, of course; but he, or she, could well have attended those classes.' He took a couple of steps and pointed to one of the prints. 'Now, this is a Stanhope Forbes.'

We both drew nearer and examined

it. A rural summer scene of children sitting on a river bank, with some old cottages beside a winding uphill road in the background.

'There *is* a similarity. Don't you think so, Quinn?' I tried to appear detached and keep the excitement out of my voice. He nodded, his gaze still on the picture.

'Those brushstrokes there, the play of light and shade, and the way the sky is portrayed, are all faintly reminiscent, I think.' Malcolm Rule nodded over the top of his glasses. 'That was painted in Hayle, we have provenance for that.'

He moved on. 'Now, this one is by Birch. He lived in Lamorna, as you probably know. He loved the place so much and made it the subject of so many of his paintings that people gave him the nickname 'Lamorna Birch', and it stuck.' He was drawing in a breath to continue, when Quinn interrupted him.

'I know Lamorna well. It's a lovely little valley leading down to the sea.'

Malcolm Rule chuckled. 'That's right. A perfect place for an artist to settle.'

While this was going on, I had been seriously studying the print. And the more I looked at it and compared it with mine, the more excited I became.

'Mr. Rule.' I cleared my throat as he turned towards me with an enquiring look. 'Don't you think this looks very much like the scene in my painting? That winding lane . . . ' As I pointed, my hand was shaking with excitement. ' . . . and the farm cottage . . . with the sea in the distance, round the bend in the road?'

He returned to his desk and picked it up, then crossed the room to compare the two. 'My dear, I do believe you could be right.' He glanced from one to the other several times. 'I don't know that Birch ever gave lessons, but it's perfectly feasible that he could have done.' He turned to me with a smile. 'Maybe even to the students at the art school.'

He drew in a breath and his shoulders lifted. 'But how you are going to find out the name of *your* artist, I've no idea.' He put into words exactly what I was thinking.

He walked back to his desk and replaced the painting. 'And that, I'm afraid, is all the help I can give you. There is so little to go on, you understand. You can, of course, go round the gallery and look at the original works. They are all here, together with others by Birch, which you could compare with this one, but apart from that . . . ' He shrugged and peered discreetly at his watch.

I took the hint and lifted the painting from the desk. Then, after thanking him profusely for his time, we did a tour of the whole gallery. I came away with a couple of catalogues to study and a lot to think about as we strolled back to the car.

5

'Lunchtime, I think.' Quinn was stowing the painting on the back seat when a nearby clock struck the hour. 'Let's go and eat. My treat,' he added with a smile.

'Oh, lovely. Thank you.' I felt a lurch of pleasure at being one of a couple for a day. It wouldn't last, of course, but to the many other pairs of young people thronging the street below, we must have seemed just like another twosome.

Quinn led the way up a street towards a café with tables outside, on a terrace overlooking the sea. My feelings were doing a see-saw between delight at having discovered a hint as to where the painting had been done, and near-despair at the mammoth task that still lay ahead.

We found a free table under an umbrella, with a magnificent view of the Mount, framed with palm trees from the nearby gardens. I sighed with contentment as I settled and we began to study our menus.

'Those fish dishes sound good,' I remarked. 'Look, Cornish bass, local crab, fresh mackerel . . . '

'Yes, I think they specialise in fish. They get it from Newlyn every morning, of course. Just a mile away. You can't beat that for freshness.' Quinn looked across and smiled.

'I'd like a crab salad,' I decided, leaning back in my chair. 'How about you?'

'I think I'll go for the mixed fish platter.' He ran his finger down the menu. 'Then I'll get a taste of everything!'

'Clever.' I smiled across the table, and noticed a couple of seagulls perched squawking on a nearby wall.

'I'm glad of this umbrella,' I remarked, glancing up. 'Beautiful as they are, those birds can be a right pest when there's food around.'

'I know. They've always got an eye

out for the main chance. They can be a right pain for people trying to eat a pasty on the beach!'

We ate in appreciative silence for a while, until Quinn pushed back his plate and sighed.

'That was delicious.' He wiped his mouth then scrunched up the napkin and discarded it. 'Yours all right, was it?'

'Oh, yes, gorgeous.' I wiped up the last of the dressing with the end of my roll and popped it into my mouth. 'That was a huge salad. I don't think I can move for a while.'

'Have you got room for a pudding to finish?' Quinn was deep in the menu again. 'They've got a wide choice.'

'Oh, I couldn't, Quinn, thanks. Just a coffee would be lovely.'

'OK.' He nodded and raised a hand for the waitress.

Replete, we were lingering over our drinks when Quinn suddenly sat forward and placed his forearms on the table.

'Alex, I think we should go to Lamorna.' He gave me a studied look. 'And see if we can find anywhere that looks remotely like the scene in your picture.'

I felt again that little frisson of pleasure as he said 'we'.

'You do?' I stared at him like a fool. 'What, today, you mean?'

'Yes, today. This afternoon. Now, in fact.' He grinned at me and leaned back in his chair again. 'I have to work tomorrow, and the rest of the week. Some of us have to earn a crust, you know.'

Looking at Quinn's smiling face, I thought how much he'd changed since I first met him. He was sitting now with his long legs stretched out beneath the table and his arms behind his head, his eyes twinkling. How he'd opened up from the serious, reticent man of few words whom I'd first met in his studio. Maybe this was what he was really like, a different man when he was away from his work and had time to relax.

But how little I really knew of Quinn.

Nothing of his background or family. Not even his full name! But just as I was going to discreetly bring up the subject, he pushed back his chair and rose to his feet.

'Come on then, let's go.' I put my thoughts on hold and followed him out of the café.

★　★　★

Up a steep hill, past isolated villages and ancient tumuli and barrows, we made our way to Lamorna.

Too intent on keeping the car on the road and negotiating the hairpin bends to talk much, Quinn was largely silent for the journey and, not wanting to distract his attention, I followed his lead. Besides, with the roof down as it was, the wind was ripping through my hair and roaring past my ears, making normal conversation impossible.

Eventually we turned off into a narrower, greener lane and began to wind downhill. There were trees here, the first we had seen since leaving Penzance, and as the lane wound gradually downwards through a scatter of cottages, I could see and hear a stream chuckling its way between mossy boulders, presumably towards the sea. Now that the car had slowed, a drift of fragrant honeysuckle scent came wafting on the breeze, and I sniffed appreciatively.

At the bottom, the lane widened and opened out at a small rocky cove with a harbour wall and a couple of brightly-painted boats anchored alongside. There was a car park, a pub and a café, and a cluster of tourists coming and going with cameras and binoculars slung around their necks. On a seat by the harbour sat a couple of elderly men in navy Guernseys and flat caps. One was smoking a pipe, the other leaning on a walking stick.

I couldn't help laughing. 'Oh Quinn, isn't that *exactly* like a seaside postcard? You can imagine the title.' I sketched quote marks in the air. ''A Typical Cornish Fishing Village'. Do you think those old men are real fishermen, or just acting the part?'

Quinn chuckled. 'Difficult to say without asking them.' We were strolling along the quay and stopped to lean over the rail. 'But fishing hasn't always been the main industry here. Quarrying was once, years and years ago. See all those huge discarded blocks up on the hill?' He pointed. 'They're left over from that time.'

'Oh, yes.' I nodded, then turned my back to the sea and looked up through the village. 'Well, here we are. Now what?' I spread my hands and shrugged. 'Where do we start?'

'Hmm.' Quinn was gazing into the middle distance with a serious expression on his face, fingering his beard. 'Well, given that those two old men look to be about a hundred, instead of laughing at them, I suggest we could ask them a few questions. About former times and people from the village. What do you think? At a guess I'd say they've always lived here, wouldn't you?'

'Oh, yes, brilliant idea! Come on.' Enthusiasm restored, I was already on my way.

There was another seat beside the one where the old men were, close enough for us to be able to strike up a conversation without it seeming too contrived.

The two heads turned to us with interest and remained staring unabashed as we sat down and settled ourselves.

'Hello.' I smiled.

'Hi.' Quinn nodded and followed my lead.

'Art'noon.' The one with the pipe removed it long enough to reply then replaced it in his mouth. Like a baby with a dummy, I thought.

'Nice day,' said Quinn.

'Ess. Handsome bit weather, innit?' the one with the stick replied. 'On holiday, are 'ee?'

Encouraged by the response, I followed it up. 'Not really. Well, only for today at least. There's something we're trying to find out, that's why we came down here.'

'Oh?' The shaggy grey eyebrows rose. 'Whass that then?'

'Well, it's quite a story.' Quinn leaned forward with his forearms on his knees and looked round me. 'Do you mind if we ask you a few questions?'

'Ask away, my bird. Don't mean ter say we'll answer em, eh Bert?' He nudged his companion with an elbow and chuckled. 'This 'ere's Bert and I'm Charlie.'

I felt obliged to reply in kind, so I said, pointing, 'This is Quinn and I'm Alex.'

'Quinn, eh?' The old man frowned and stared. 'What sort of a name do 'ee call that then? Short for summat, is it?'

I glanced at Quinn, waiting for his reaction. 'Yeah, sort of.' He shifted his position and looked slightly embarrassed, but did not expound.

'Well, anyway, what can us do fer 'ee?' Charlie asked.

Quinn turned to me to take the lead, so I cleared my throat and took in a breath. 'Well, I've got this painting, you see, that's quite old.' I drew it out of my big shoulder-bag. It was actually the case for my laptop, but I'd found it to be the ideal size for this purpose.

'Someone told me it might have been painted around here, many years ago.' I passed it over and he took it between two bent and gnarled hands.

'Excuse me asking — ' This was an afterthought. ' — but have you always lived in this village? Long enough to remember what it used to be like?'

'Lived here all me life, maid. Lamorna born and bred, I am. Bert here, though, he's a newcomer. Awnly bin 'ere sixty years, Bert have.' He chortled and the stooped shoulders heaved with merriment.

'Then, I wonder whether you would have known . . . ' I took in a breath. 'Charlie, do you remember an artist called Samuel Birch who used to live here? They called him 'Lamorna Birch'. It would have been in the nineteen-hundreds. You would have been a young man then, wouldn't you?'

'Mr. Birch? Aw, 'ess. Remember him well. Nice bloke he were.' Charlie shifted in his seat and looked over his shoulder. 'Lived in that house up there, he did. Used to be the harbourmaster's place.' He nodded, sunk in reminiscence. 'Ess, he were always around the place with his easel and his paints. Not half bad his stuff was, too.'

I smiled at this appraisal of one of the period's most famous artists; then, catching sight of Quinn's amused expression, I tried not to burst out laughing.

'Do you know if he ever gave lessons to other people as well? Students, you know?' I straightened my face and tried to concentrate.

'Dunno, my handsome, couldn't tell 'ee, I'm sure.' Charlie shrugged his bent shoulders and coughed. 'I do remember un getting us children to pose for his pictures though. Give us sixpence he would, to sit by the river, or on a hedge or summat, while he painted the view. I never did, couldn't sit still long enough, but he had some of the girls queueing up for un. Showing off like, they was, tickled pink to be put in a picture.' He nodded and fell silent, sunk in recollections of his lost youth. Then he straightened and nudged Bert's elbow.

''Ere, Bert, remember that Louisa, do 'ee, and that friend of hers, um . . . her name's gone, but you d'know who I mean. They was always together as young 'uns, and they used to follow Mr. Birch around when he was painting, hoping he'd put them in a picture. They were some lively pair, they two. Used to get up to some mischief later on too, chasing the boys and all. Remember, do 'ee?'

'Aw, 'ess. You d' mean Nellie . . . Nellie . . . ' He shook his head. 'Something.'

'*Nell*. Thass right.' He gave his friend a shrewd look, then turned to us and winked. 'Had a soft spot for her yourself once, didn't 'ee, Bert?' he chuckled.

Bert hurrumphed into his beard and made no reply. Instead, he took the painting from Charlie and peered at it.

'Well, less 'ave another look at this 'ere, shall us?'

There followed a period of silence broken only by the occasional wheezy breath and a grunt of concentration as the two scrutinised the picture.

I sat back and waited, enjoying the sun on my face and the scent of salt and seaweed on the air. The water swelled and slopped in the harbour at our feet and overhead, gulls wheeled and screeched, tossing like scraps of paper in the stiff onshore wind. Where the sun caught their darting wings they were turned to birds of silver, then back to snow-white. They looked unearthly, elemental, spirits of air.

Then the spell was broken as Bert moved, reaching into a pocket to pull out a pair of glasses. 'Dang me, can't see so good these days without these on me nose,' he muttered. 'Make me feel like an old man, they do.'

Quinn and I both curled up at the same time and tried to hide our laughter with a fit of coughing. When we could speak again he said, 'Do you mind me asking how old you two actually are? If it wouldn't be too cheeky.'

'Nar, thass all right.' Bert squinted at him over the top of his specs. 'Eighty-five I am. Charlie's what . . . ninety-two, are 'ee, Charlie? Ninety-three is it?'

'Ninety-three next Christmas, I'll be, if I'm spared.' He drew in a breath then started muttering to himself. 'Well, bless my soul, look at that. If that idn' . . . 'tis though . . . 'tis too. Here Bert, look at this. What would you say that there place were? That house. Recognise un, do 'ee?' He tapped the canvas with a swollen, arthritic finger.

'Give it here boy, less have a closer look.' Bert put out a brawny hand and held the picture up to his eyes.

'Chycarn Farm, innit? Look like. Up the end of the lane. Only, like it did use to be. Not now. All holiday lets these days, 'tis.' He grunted and sighed. 'They handsome out buildings all done out with plastic windows, a gurt swimming pool where the mowhay used ter be and the fields all sold off. Crying shame I do call it, but thass progress, so they say.' The two old heads nodded in unison.

My heart had lurched at hearing the name of the farm, and as Quinn's gaze flipped to meet mine, I knew he was thinking the same thing: that maybe we were getting somewhere at last.

After thanking the two old men for their enormous help, we left them to their reminiscences and set off in the direction they'd indicated. The former farm was, apparently, 'Uplong a bit and on yer left.'

As we walked back the way we had come, it was easy enough to see the notice announcing 'Chycarn Holiday Accommodation' that we had failed to spot when driving down.

I was still clutching hold of the picture that I hadn't put away since Charlie handed it back. 'Quinn, before we go in there, let's see if we can find the exact spot where the artist was standing when this was painted.' I flourished it in his face.

'Yes, sure, if you want to.' He took a quick glance at it, then stopped and gazed around. 'We need to be further up the road. Look — ' He pointed. ' — the painter was viewing the farm more from above. And angled a bit to his or her right.'

'That's it. So it is.' I followed his line of sight and started moving again. 'Come on. Over this way.'

When we came to a granite stile set in the hedge, Quinn stopped and pointed. 'Now, I think we need to go over that. There's a pathway through those fields, see it?'

The stile was quite a challenge and I was glad I was wearing jeans. There were three huge steps and a block across the top, with three more steps down the other side. Quinn with his long legs was over it in a flash, then he turned to hold out a hand to me.

I had no choice but to take it. To insist I could manage without would seem unfriendly. Besides, the truth was,

I couldn't. Not gracefully, anyway. And there were tall nettles and brambles growing between the stones, too.

So I put the painting back into my large bag and slipped my fingers into his. He grasped them firmly and hauled me to the top. That was fine. As I teetered on the uneven step, though, our eyes met. We were on the same level now, and for a moment, as I gazed into Quinn's face, time seemed to stand still. There were little creases at the corners of his eyes where he was screwing them up against the sun, and the breeze was lifting his wavy hair, blowing it up the wrong way. I had to forcibly resist the urge to smooth it down, stroke it back from his face . . . Forgetting my precarious perch, I gasped as I started wobbling.

Then every breath left my body as he withdrew the hand, put both arms to my waist and lifted me down, giving me a little twirl as he set me on my feet.

Quinn immediately set off across the field as if nothing out of the ordinary had happened at all. Well, of course, to him it wouldn't have done, would it? It was only me who was reacting like some moonstruck teenager. But I could still feel the strength of those taut muscles against my heart, and the warmth where his arms had been around me. I scowled and stomped through the long grass in his wake, feeling hot and foolish.

I gave my full attention to the job in hand and took another swift glimpse into the bag at the painting. Then as I glanced back the way we'd just come, a thought struck me and I called out to his retreating back. 'Quinn! Stop! We've come too far.' He turned and glanced back over his shoulder.

'Look at this.' I pointed towards the stile and as he reached my side I took the painting back out and showed him. 'I think we passed the spot we're searching for without noticing it. If you come back to the stile . . . ' I was leading the way as I spoke. ' . . . can you see? The person was sitting on it.

Or on the hedge nearby. It fits the angle exactly.' My pointing finger trembled with excitement.

'So it does! Well done. You clever girl!' Quinn beamed at me and clapped me on the shoulder. I decided to ignore the faint hint of condescension in his tone, and returned the grin.

'I do want to take some photos of the scene as it is now.' I rummaged for my camera.

This time I managed the steps for myself: they were easier from this side. Then I sat on the top one to take the photos and scrambled down the other side with no problems.

'So all we need to do now — ' Quinn paused as we rejoined the road. ' — is find out who your painter was.'

I sighed. 'Yes. That's 'all'. Well, we'd better call at Chycarn Holiday Accommodation, I suppose, and see if we can come up with anything there.'

'Unlikely, I'd say; but yes, OK, if you want to.'

Quinn heaved a sigh. I glanced

sideways at him, alerted by his negative tone of voice, and saw him glance at his watch. 'Quinn,' I said tentatively, 'are you getting fed up with all this?' I paused and swallowed. 'Because I'd understand if you were, and I'm immensely grateful to you for coming all this way with me . . . '

'No, that's all right. I've really enjoyed it.' He ran a hand through his hair, leaving it sticking up in tufts. 'Only, we've taken longer than I thought. I need to get back soon. I've got an arrangement for this evening, you see.'

I felt a stab of contrition as I realised how long we'd been out. 'Oh, of *course*. Why didn't you mention it sooner?'

'As I said, I was enjoying it. But if you don't mind . . . '

'We'll leave right away. I can always come down again with Sue. She'd love it. So many opportunities for gorgeous photos. Even Bert and Charlie would make a fantastic picture, wouldn't they? She could call it 'Local Colour'.'

I was babbling away and waving my hands about as I led the way to the car. It covered the faint embarrassment I was feeling, but mostly the curiosity. Who had Quinn arranged to meet that evening? Was it a girl? He wasn't likely to tell me, and I could hardly ask, but I was longing to know. Sternly, I told myself to mind my own business. I arrived at the car park out of breath, and irritable that the lovely day was to end so abruptly.

The journey back was made in near-silence. Even if the rushing wind hadn't made conversation too difficult, I sensed that Quinn was sunk as deep in his own thoughts as I was, and a distance seemed to have crept in between us. We parted with a few polite remarks and my renewed thanks for his help.

6

Sue was sitting with her feet up on the sofa as I let myself in, poring over her camera.

'Hi Alex.' She swung her legs down and made room for me. 'Had a good day? Did you find out anything?' Her eyes were sparkling, her face flushed by the sun and wind, and she seemed even more bubbly than usual.

'Yes, I have; and yes, I did.' I set down my bag and joined her. 'You look as if you've enjoyed yourself, too.'

'Yes, I did.' A thoughtful expression on her face, she added, 'I met this interesting man . . . '

I tried to keep a straight face. 'Oh?'

'Yes. He was out walking too, with his dog. The dog bounded up to me and I was stroking it when he came up and apologised for it bothering me. We had a bit of a chat. He's on a walking holiday. Then funnily enough, I met him again in a little pub where I stopped for a cup of tea. In a village somewhere out in the wilds. I can't remember the name, but it began with Z.'

'Oh, yes.' Preoccupied with my own thoughts, my reply was a bit vague. The truth was, the subjects of my painting and Quinn were never far from my mind, but until Sue had gone back I couldn't really spend all my time obsessed with my own concerns. It wouldn't be fair to her. But thinking of the painting had reminded me that I had promised myself I'd spend much of the summer weather out sketching. Only up to now I hadn't done a single thing about it.

* * *

'How about going to that exhibition at the Tate tomorrow?' Sue's voice broke into my train of thought. We were sitting outside in the tiny back yard of the cottage on sun-loungers, catching the last of the day's warmth, when she put aside the paperback she'd been reading and swung her legs to the ground. 'What do you think?'

'Well, I'm torn between doing that and going sketching.' I pushed my sunglasses up to the top of my head. I'd been watching the world go by below us and for once doing absolutely nothing. 'While the weather holds I ought to make the most of it.'

She shrugged and gave a little sigh. 'Oh, right.' Knowing her so well, I could hear the note of disappointment in her voice.

'We could do the Tate in the morning, though.' I did a bit of quick thinking. 'Then go sight-seeing somewhere in the afternoon, and I'll take my sketching things too. How would that be?'

Sue's face brightened. 'Lovely. Let's do that, if you're sure. Where shall we go?'

Eventually, after a long discussion, we decided on Land's End. We agreed that she couldn't be as close as we were and not see the famous place. So we drove right around the peninsula, stood at the end of the country, and she marvelled with countless others at the vast expanse of Atlantic Ocean sweeping away to the distant horizon.

I was hoping on the way back to get a closer look at some of the ancient standing stones I remembered from coming here as a child with Grandma. So, while Sue went off with her camera, I puffed my way up a steep hill — where, according to the map, I should find an ancient fortification called Chun Castle, and one of the quoits.

And there they were. There was very little left of what had once been the castle. A recognisable gateway and the quoit nearby, with its three tall pillars and a capstone. The capstone, however, had slipped from its original position over the ages, and now stood tip-tilted at an angle, propped against the others.

As I paused to get my breath back, I turned and looked back the way I'd come. From this height the view was awesome. Gigantic boulders tumbled across the open moorland towards the unbelievably blue sea. If it weren't for the little crofts and smallholdings dotted here and there, it would have remained unchanged since the ancient people had lived here and built this enormous edifice.

I perched myself on a flat rock and was soon absorbed in my work. My pencil flew over the paper as I concentrated on getting as much of it down as I could, before Sue came back.

When she did return much later, the sun was going down, my fingers were aching and so were my eyes. Sue was even more weary than I, having walked further. But elated, too, by the wonderful scenery she had captured on her camera.

We went back to the cottage, but even after I'd washed and changed I couldn't really relax. Thoughts of Quinn kept surfacing in the most irritating way. I couldn't get him out of my mind. He was so different from my former husband in every way. Sensitive, caring and reticent. Too reticent in some ways. How could he be so friendly and helpful, yet still keep his real self so private? Apart from what showed on the surface, I knew little more about the man than when I first met him. I felt on edge and couldn't get interested in anything.

'I think I'll go for a stroll across the beach, Sue, before I settle.' I rose to my feet and tossed aside the magazine I was pretending to read.

'Oh, fine. Can I come too, or would you rather be on your own?'

'No, no, that's all right, if you're not too tired. Let's both go.' I glanced out of the window as I crossed the room. 'Oh, look at that glorious sunset!' The sky was alight with dramatic shades of flame and lemon, streaked with bars of pearl grey, as the dying sun put on its last display of colour before sinking into the sea.

We were strolling along the harbour

front when a burst of music and the sound of singing came floating out of the open door of The Sloop.

'Shall we go in and see what's going on?' Pausing for a moment, I laid a hand on Sue's arm and jerked my head in the direction of the pub. I needed a diversion to take me out of myself.

'OK. Why not? I quite fancy a drink.' We changed direction and threaded our way through the people drinking outside and into the sudden dimness.

In a corner, beneath the low beams and blackened rafters, a group of about half a dozen men were singing around a piano. Folk songs, and the audience was joining in the rousing choruses with great gusto.

We were pushing our way to the bar when Sue, who was in front, stopped suddenly as someone spoke to her. It was difficult to hear what she was saying above the din, but as I drew closer a young man rose to his feet and held out a hand to me.

'Alex, this is John Champion. What a

coincidence — do you remember I told you about the walker I met the other morning?'

'Down at Zennor,' he added as we shook hands.

'Zennor! Yes. I couldn't remember the name when I got back.' Sue turned to him in explanation. Tall, blond and suntanned, with a neatly-trimmed beard, John smiled at us both.

'What will you have?' he asked, nodding towards the bar.

'Oh, no, you mustn't,' I murmured, in a brief lull between choruses.

'Nonsense, of course I will.' He brushed aside both our protestations and indicated that we should sit at his table so it wouldn't be taken.

My back was to the bar, and until John returned with the drinks I didn't notice he wasn't alone. I looked over my shoulder and smiled my thanks as he put a glass in front of me. Then my eyes met those of the person who had been so much a part of my thoughts that it seemed as if I'd conjured him up.

It was Quinn, of course, and I felt warmth rise to my cheeks in the most irritating way.

I would have preferred not to meet him socially, especially in front of Sue, who never missed a thing. She knew me so well, I felt sure she would notice my reaction and jump to conclusions. It would be just like her. But there was nothing I could do about that.

I smiled automatically as John made the introductions. 'This is my friend, Quinn,' he said. 'We go back a long way, although I no longer live in Cornwall.' He turned to Sue and me, explaining. 'I come back every summer if I can, to walk the coastal path. I love this area.' He waved a hand expressively and glanced out of the window. 'We arrange to have a drink together in the same place on the same date every year, if we can. That was yesterday. Then tonight we met here quite by chance.'

Then the penny dropped. So, this was the 'arrangement' Quinn had meant when he said he had to get back from Lamorna. Not a girl, then. My spirits rose. Although, conversely, I was now wondering why he *didn't* appear to have one.

'Actually, we've met already,' I murmured and John's brows rose. Quinn folded his long legs into the small space available and nodded.

'Yes. On business.' Quinn picked up his drink and took a sip, looking at me over the rim of his glass. His mouth quirked with the ghost of a smile and I smiled broadly back.

'Oh, you're the picture framer, aren't you?' Sue smiled. 'I remember the notice over the door of your studio. Is Quinn your first or second name?'

He was gazing at the tabletop and absently drew a finger through the damp ring made by his glass. 'Oh, my surname's Nancarrow,' he replied absently.

Just then the singers launched into a rousing song about someone called Trelawny, and conversation became impossible. It went on for several verses, and John started joining in the choruses about 'twenty thousand Cornishmen' with gusto, thumping on the table with a fist to add to the noise.

'That's the nearest thing there is to a Cornish national anthem,' he explained when it became possible to speak again. 'So I've been told.'

'*National* anthem? Don't you mean 'county'?' Sue's eyes widened. 'Cornwall's hardly a country!'

'Ah.' Quinn sat back and regarded us all. 'I suppose you don't know that many local people consider Cornwall to be a separate nation? Like Wales. It has an ancient culture and history of its own, and we're very proud of it.'

'So who was this Trelawny chap, then?' John took a swig from his glass and looked expectantly towards Quinn.

'He's the county's favourite folk hero.' Quinn chuckled. 'Although there never was a march to London like in the song. He was a bishop. Bishop Trelawny. It was during the reign of King James the Second. He refused to read the Declaration of Indulgence in his diocese.'

'The *what?*' Sue interrupted, leaning forward and with a frown.

'It was a proclamation granting tolerance towards Roman Catholics. He didn't agree with it. So he was imprisoned in the Tower and put on trial with six other bishops. Eventually they were all acquitted.' Quinn sat back and folded his arms.

'Oh.' Sue stared at him. 'I've never heard of him.' She glanced towards me. 'I suppose you have, Alex?'

'Of course I have. Grandma had a book of Cornish history. I read it as a child.'

The noise level now was so high we could hardly hear ourselves speak. I glanced over my shoulder at the group around the piano, who had launched into another, slightly more bawdy, folk song.

'It's a stag night do,' Quinn said. 'That chap in the blue shirt's getting married on Saturday.'

John chuckled. 'I can still remember your stag night, Quinn, can't you? Up in London, that was,' he said in a brief aside to Sue and me. 'It was quite something. I nearly had to fish him out of a fountain in Trafalgar Square on the way back. He was due to marry Caroline the following morning, you see, and we'd stopped to sober him up in the water. That's when he nearly fell in.'

'That was a long time ago, mate. Like another lifetime, now.' Quinn upended his glass and wiped his mouth with the back of one hand.

I was feeling as if a black hole had suddenly opened up and swallowed me. The raucous music, chatter and laughter receded, leaving me inside my own head, numb, reeling from the shock. Quinn — *married*! All sorts of questions were whirling around in my mind. Why had he never mentioned her? Where was she? Why had I never seen the slightest hint of a woman in his life? After all the time we'd spent together and . . .

As someone spoke to me, I was

instantly back in the pub again, feeling as if a vast amount of time had passed, but it could only have been seconds. I turned to Sue, who was asking if I wanted another drink.

I shook my head and summoned up a smile. 'Oh, no thanks. I haven't finished this one yet.'

'Are you all right, Alex?' She stared at me in concern. 'You're looking ever so pale.'

'I'm OK. Bit of a headache, that's all.' I raised a hand to my forehead.

'No wonder, in all this racket.' She turned away as Quinn spoke.

'So, what have you two been doing today?' He put down his glass and leaned back with an inquiring glance towards me.

But Sue replied before I had to. 'Oh, we've been down to Land's End this afternoon. Very impressive. Fantastic scenery. I took some really good shots and Alex did a lot of sketches.' She swirled her drink and took a sip.

After a little more small talk and a

visit to the toilet, I used the headache
— which had now become reality — as
an excuse to leave. Sue joined me as
we said our goodbyes and stepped out
into the fresh air, which felt marvellous
after the stuffy room.

In front of us just across the road the
water in the harbour was calm and still,
glowing a fabulous shade of turquoise
in the evening light. As we left the pub,
coloured boats were bobbing gently at
their moorings and there was scarcely a
breath of wind to ruffle the surface.

'John's asked me if I'd like to go for a
walk tomorrow,' Sue said as we were
strolling slowly homeward.

'Oh? And are you going to?' She
didn't meet my eyes as I spoke. Her
hands thrust into the pockets of her
shorts, she was looking fixedly at the
cobbles at our feet.

'Mm, yes, I am.' Sue nodded and
looked up. 'He suggested going over to
Gwithian and . . . um . . . Godrevy, I
think it was. Where the lighthouse is.'

'That's nice. You'll enjoy that.' I

glanced sideways at her. 'You like John, don't you?'

She nodded again. 'Yes, he's a really nice guy. We get on well.'

'And I suppose you won't ever see him again once you leave here, will you?' I was fishing, wondering if John was going to be just another of Sue's 'pebbles on the beach'.

We turned up the steps to the cottage and I stopped to rummage for the key.

'Actually, we've arranged to meet again when we both get back.' She turned to me, suddenly animated, and started waving her hands about. 'Alex, it's the most amazing coincidence, but we've discovered John lives not far from me!'

She paused in the hall, and now I could see her flushed face and the sparkle in her eyes.

'He has a house in Bromley, which is really not far away from me in Beckenham. We're on the same bus route!'

'And he's single?' I enquired casually, wondering if she was getting herself into complications again.

'Oh yes, he says he's been a confirmed bachelor all his life — until he met me!' Sue was staring dreamily at nothing, lost in her own private world. I felt a little stab of — what? Envy? Which vanished as suddenly as it had come.

'Well, I really hope it all works out for you both.' I gave her a hug as we entered the kitchen and set about finding something for us to eat.

'So you'll be out all day,' I said thoughtfully, through a mouthful of chicken pie, 'and you won't be using your car if John's picking you up, will you?'

'That's right. Why? Do you want to borrow it?'

'Could I? Because I've just had a thought. It would be brilliant if you're agreeable. I could get back to Lamorna, you see, and carry on the search where Quinn and I left off. He's tied up with work at the moment, so I'm going on by myself.'

'Of course you can.' Sue smiled at me over the rim of her mug. 'Good idea. Then I shan't feel so guilty at leaving you on your own.'

7

Sue and John were off early, and as soon as I'd cleared up and got myself organised, I set off in Sue's little blue Fiat. The weather forecast wasn't too good — there was a hint of drizzle coming over in the late afternoon — so I mentally crossed my fingers for us all as I turned down the remembered road to Lamorna.

It felt strange to be on my own. I felt Quinn's shadow reflecting mine as I parked the car and looked around. I remembered the disappointment I'd felt when we'd parted that day, and sternly I told myself not to be such a fool.

There was no sign of Bert or Charlie today as I glanced towards the harbour, which was rather disappointing, but there was a cool breeze coming off the sea and it was probably too cold for them. However, the village was just as charming, and I set off up the road to the farm.

I was trying to control my excitement, but I couldn't suppress a flutter of nerves as I approached the old farmhouse. It had been done up, as Bert had said, with double-glazing and colourful window boxes. The thatch had been replaced by a conventional roof, obviously a long time ago judging by the orange lichen softening its grey slates. I pushed open the door that had a sign on it saying 'Reception'.

'Good morning.' A pleasant-faced woman in her late fifties, maybe sixty, was sitting at a computer station, and turned her head as I entered. She rose with a smile and came forward to the counter. A rack stuffed with leaflets advertising local attractions stood to one side of it, flanked by another holding postcards. 'How can I help you? We do have some vacancies.'

I smiled as I returned her greeting. 'Oh, no, it's not about booking. I'm wondering if you could possibly help me with something else.' I told her my story and, withdrawing the painting from my bag, laid it on the counter in front of her.

'This is how your farm looked in 1935, the date on the back of the painting. And I'm trying to find out who the artist was.'

I paused for breath as she carefully picked up the painting and held it out in front of her. Small and neat-featured, she was wearing a slim denim skirt with a checked shirt tucked into it beneath a leather belt.

'Oh, my goodness!' Her eyebrows shot up and she glanced quickly up at me, seeming more surprised than I had expected. 'Look, you'd better come through.' She lifted the flap of the counter. 'I'm Philippa, by the way.' She held out a hand and I introduced myself.

'There's someone you must met. Come this way.' Intrigued, I followed Philippa down the passage towards the back of the house. 'The farm has been in our family since long before the 1930s, I know.' She gestured with a hand. 'We've only recently turned it into holiday lets. We've had to diversify, like lots of other farmers.' She spoke over her shoulder. 'The business brings in more money this way than farming ever would today.'

She paused to open a door and ushered me into a high-ceilinged room with elaborate cornices and a plaster moulding surrounding the central light fitting. One wall was of natural stone with a large fireplace set in it, the others painted in a restful pale green. At the far end a modern conservatory had been added, with double doors leading out onto a patio. The room was a tasteful, comfortable blend of old and new. And, seated in a deep armchair bolstered with several cushions, facing the garden, was a very old woman.

'This is Gran.' Philippa gestured with a hand as we crossed the room. 'She's ninety-five and, apart from being slightly hard of hearing, is as brisk and lively as many ten years younger.'

She bent over the old lady and gained her attention. 'Hello Gran. All right, are you? Here's a surprise, look. A visitor for you.'

'Gran' turned in her chair and peered over her shoulder, laying aside the crocheting she had been busy with. 'Visitor? Who . . . ?'

'A young lady. This is Alex.' She drew me forward. 'She wants to talk to you about the old days. You'll like that, won't you?'

She indicated a cane chair where I could sit and pulled up another for herself. 'This is my grandmother, Louisa Viant.'

'Pleased to meet you, my dear. You must call me Granny Lou like everyone else does. Never was one for standing on ceremony.'

A welcoming smile deepened the creases in her lined face, a face as crinkled as a walnut, while two brown eyes as bright as a robin's regarded me with interest. She extended a hand and

I gently grasped it. Hers was knotted and gnarled, the knuckles twisted with possible arthritis, but showed unexpected strength in its grip.

I smiled into the bright eyes as we sat down and she regarded me intently. 'So where do you come from, my handsome? Don't live round here, do you? I know most people in the village and there 'idden no family called Rowe down here.'

'Oh, I live a long way away from here,' I said with a laugh. 'Right over to St. Ives.' The old lady chuckled.

Quinn's face came into my mind as I spoke. Never very far away from my thoughts, how I would have liked him to be here today to see the continuation of our search. But . . . I shook myself back to the present as Philippa spoke.

'Alex has brought something to show you, Gran.' She sat forward and pointed to the picture on my lap.

I held it up for her to see. 'Yes. This is a painting that's been in my family for years. It belonged to my Grandma, but

I don't know anything about it. I came here to see if I could find out who the artist was. The name of the farm is on the back, and somebody told me the place looked like Lamorna . . . ' I simplified the story and omitted the stuff about the art gallery. This was enough for such an elderly person to cope with.

' . . . So here I am. And I recognised the farm immediately, although so much has changed.'

But I could tell the old lady was only half-listening. She was looking at Philippa with the same expression of amazement I'd seen before.

'Show her, Pippa,' she said, prising herself out of the chair and rising to her feet. Her granddaughter passed her a walking stick that was hanging on the back of it, and extended an arm to help her up.

'We're going down to the kitchen,' Philippa called over her shoulder as we left the room. 'This way. You'll see why in a minute.' I gave a mental shrug. I'd no idea what to expect.

The room we entered was a typical farmhouse kitchen, only slightly modernised by the Aga where the Cornish range would have been, and the double-glazed windows. What drew my attention like a magnet, however, were a couple of paintings on the far wall.

'There.' Louisa sank into an easy-chair and pointed with her stick. 'Take a look at those, dear. What do you think of them, eh?'

I drew in a breath, feeling my eyes widen. These were so similar in style to my own that they just had to be by the same artist. Two more views of the farm. I felt my mouth opening as I turned to Philippa in amazement. She smiled as I stepped nearer.

One of them showed cattle grazing contentedly in a lush meadow edged with tall trees, a glimpse of the sea in the distance and a corner of the house in the foreground. The other was a picture of a young girl in a long skirt and white pinafore, a straw hat hanging down her back by its elastic. She was standing on the bottom rail of a fence, stroking the nose of a white pony.

'That girl was my dearest friend.' The old lady pointed. 'She was fifteen years old when I painted that picture.' She turned back to face me and paused. 'And I was seventeen.'

I felt as if that pony had kicked me in the stomach. '*You* painted it? *Really?*' I felt my jaw drop. 'B . . . but . . . they are both so like mine!' The truth hit me with the force of a whirlwind. 'So, if . . . if *you* were that artist, you must have painted . . . this one?' I pointed with a hand that shook.

Louisa nodded, and I noticed her eyes were damp. 'I can't imagine how you come to have it, my handsome, but I gave it to Nell for her birthday once. Well, Eleanor was her proper name, but she was always Nell to me. We were friends all our lives, right from childhood.'

Her voice sank to a whisper. 'She died young, though. I still miss her, even now.' Lost in melancholy for a moment, the expression on her face touched something in me, and I felt a lump in my own throat.

'*Eleanor!*' My stomach did a flip as the name sank in. 'That was my great-grandmother's name!' I blurted.

'What did you say?' Philippa leaned forward, her forehead creasing.

'The picture came to me from my grandmother. And her mother was called Eleanor — or Nell.' I saw the astonishment reflected on Philippa's face as well, as our glances met.

'What was her surname?' Philippa asked, wide-eyed. 'Her maiden name of course, that would be.'

When I told her, she gave a gasp of astonishment, and tears had begun rolling down the old lady's face now.

'Oh, how wonderful!' She clasped my hands with both of hers. 'To think you are part of Nell's family! I can hardly believe it.' She continued to look deeply into my face. 'So the girl with the pony — ' She pointed to the painting.

' — is your great-grandmother. Well, well!'

I nodded as a lump came to my throat and I swallowed hard.

'I never met her, of course, and my grandmother didn't talk a lot about her past. She certainly didn't tell me who painted her picture; but then, I never asked. I've just always loved it.' I gently withdrew from the old lady's clasp and she sank back against the cushions of her chair.

'And what a coincidence,' Philippa broke in, 'that the picture should come back here, where it was painted, after all these years.'

Granny Lou wiped the back of her hand across her eyes. 'I'm a sentimental old fool, maid, but I'm so glad it's gone to someone who cherishes it, as you obviously do.'

I was nearly in tears myself by now, the room was charged with so much emotion. 'Oh, yes, I always will. Especially now I know the story behind it.'

I was trying to think of some way of lightening the atmosphere. So I deliberately fixed a smile on my face and changed the subject. 'I met two old fishermen down on the quay the other day, who said they knew you when you were girls, you and Nell.'

A broad smile spread across her wrinkled features and her eyes began to sparkle again. 'Oh, that would be Bert and Charlie, I suppose.'

I nodded and smiled. 'They said you were a pair of bright young things in those days. Following Mr. Birch the artist around, and asking to be put in his pictures.'

She chuckled softly. 'Oh, yes. That would have been Nell more than me. My father was an artist too, and a friend of Mr. Birch. I only wanted to watch. To learn from real artists. How to do it, how to make beautiful pictures like they did.' She sighed. 'And I did learn, such a lot, but of course I was never anywhere near as good.'

'But these are wonderful!' I waved a

hand to indicate the paintings on the wall. 'You're just being too modest.'

'She always did run herself down,' Philippa said. 'Never thought her work was any good. I'm always telling her.' She smiled fondly at the old lady.

By this time, however, I could see that Granny Lou was sagging in her chair from exhaustion. I was feeling wrung out myself by all the excitement. But at last I'd found the answer to the mystery of my painting. And Great-Grandmother Eleanor had emerged as a real person, no longer just a name lost in the distant past.

'I'll take Gran up for her nap.' Philippa rose to her feet. 'Come on Gran, time for a lie-down. Perhaps Alex will come to visit again sometime?' She turned enquiringly to me.

'Oh, *yes*. I'd love to. And I'll see myself out, don't you bother. I'll phone and let you know when I'm coming again, shall I? I've got the number here.' I showed her one of the business cards I'd picked up from the desk when I came in. She nodded and raised a hand as I turned to go.

And for once I didn't pay much attention to the scenery during my journey back.

8

Sue was home before me and already had a meal waiting. 'Oh, wonderful, you're a star,' I said as I sniffed the savoury smells on the air.

'It's only pasta, but I'm so ravenous I did the quickest thing I could think of.'

'Lovely. Did you have a good walk?' I tossed my bag onto a chair and raked my fingers through my hair. 'Sometimes I think I'll cut all this short like yours,' I remarked, glancing in the mirror at my windblown tangles.

'No-o, don't. It suits you.' Sue turned from the cooker, spoon in hand. 'Especially with your dark eyes.'

She paused, twirling the spoon as she gazed out of the window. 'Walk? Oh, yes, I should say so. We walked it seemed like *miles* along the cliffs to get to this place, but John said it wasn't very far and that I'm just out of practice. Of course, he thinks nothing of a ten-mile hike, so to him it probably wasn't. Far, I mean.' She smiled and shrugged. 'My feet are aching like anything. I think I'll have a bath and an early night. And how was your day? Did you find out anything about your picture?'

She put two steaming bowls on the table and I sat down with a sigh of contentment. 'Oh, yes, I certainly did.'

And I proceeded to tell her the whole tale from start to finish.

★ ★ ★

We spent the next day exploring the north Cornwall coast: walking the wide beaches of Perranporth and Newquay, at this time of year thronged with holidaymakers; then all the way up to Padstow and the estuary of the river Camel.

But soon Saturday dawned and it was time to say goodbye to Sue. 'It's been a marvellous week, Alex, and there is still so much else I'd love to see and do.

We've hardly touched the south coast, have we?' She grinned. 'And yes, I'm fishing for another invitation.'

'For goodness' sake — you don't have to fish,' I retorted. 'You know you're perfectly welcome any time. I shan't be going anywhere in a hurry.'

I wondered momentarily what I *was* going to do next. The shock of having my life turned upside down in such a comparatively short space of time had left me mentally numb.

I had really enjoyed Sue's company — it had kept me from thinking about myself — and we parted with promises to keep in touch, and a return open invitation for me to go and stay with her at any time.

I waved her off, and kept waving until the little car was out of sight, then shut the door and sat down in the quiet house. Now I could collect my thoughts and proceed with my plans for the painting. Which meant going over to see Quinn and telling him all about the momentous story I'd uncovered. And to be aware always that we were friends and could be nothing more. Ever.

So, with mixed feelings — for it meant I would at last have to give it up once I'd had the photo taken — I picked up my bag containing the picture and set off for the craft studios. I could well have asked Sue to do the photograph, but I wanted it to be as perfect as possible, and that meant a professional job.

There were a couple of customers in Quinn's studio, so I hung about in the passage, studying the pieces on display as I waited, and keeping an eye on what was going on inside.

I could hear from their accents that the couple were Americans, and that they were very taken with Quinn's work. They must have been coming to the end of their visit, as I could see that he was putting aside more than one article on the counter between them. Money changed hands and then they were leaving. As I heard them making arrangements for their purchases to be collected later, I moved to one side until they had made their way out into the street, then slipped into the studio.

'Alex! Hello.' He was still standing behind the counter, with both hands resting on it, smiling broadly.

'Hi Quinn. I saw your customers. They looked as if they'd bought a few things.'

His face still wreathed in smiles, he nodded. 'They certainly did. It was the best sale I've had for ages. A coffee table, a three-legged stool and the carved eagle, as you can see.' He nodded towards the group at my feet.

'Wonderful! I'm really pleased for you.'

'Come on through.' Quinn led the way into the inner room and indicated a seat. 'Cup of coffee?' He moved towards the kettle that he kept on a corner shelf. I nodded. 'Please.'

He pushed a mugful towards me when it was ready and sank into a chair. 'And what about you? Has your friend gone back yet?'

'Yes, just this morning. Oh, Quinn, I've got so much to tell you I hardly know where to begin. I went back to Lamorna, you see . . . ' Taking a deep breath I launched into the whole tale as we sipped our coffee and the world went by outside.

' . . . then to find that the artist was such a close friend of my own great-grandmother! It was amazing.'

I felt a lump rise to my throat as my eyes misted over. 'And what a pity that Granny Lou's too old to paint the copy for me,' I said wistfully. 'That would make a perfect ending.'

Quinn's eyes had hardly left my face as he sat taking it all in, and he hadn't spoken a word until my voice tailed off as I finished. Now he let out a breath and ran a hand through his thick mop of hair.

'Phew! What a fantastic story, Alex! Fancy finding out all you wanted to know, and more besides, in just one visit. Great.' He beamed at me. 'So, now you're ready to keep your side of our bargain, of course, and let me get to work on that painting of yours at last.'

I lifted a hand to interrupt him. 'There's just one more thing to do, Quinn, don't forget. I need a good photograph of it, so I can get the copy painted.'

'Oh, yes.' He nodded vigorously. 'Well, that's easily done. You must go and see Eve. You won't have to go any further than the studio just round the corner. She's been here for years and is very highly thought of.'

'Oh, good. All right, I will. But I want to make sure I have a *really* good photo before you set about scraping off my painting, so don't think you're going to lay your hands on it for a day or two.' I laughed, but I meant what I said. I wanted a perfect replica before my original vanished for ever.

'Of course. Give me a call when you're ready. There's the number.' He jerked a thumb towards a stack of his business cards at my elbow.

'OK.' And a small silence fell as we

sipped our coffee, lost in our own thoughts.

I picked up one of the cards and twiddled it absent-mindedly. Then the thought occurred to me that here was an opportunity to find out what I wanted to know.

'Yours is a very unusual first name, Quinn. I don't recall hearing it before. Where does it come from? Is it short for something?'

'Ah, sorry Alex.' He shook his head and his tone was gruff. 'I can't tell you that one.' He looked down and swirled his coffee. 'There's a story attached to it that I only tell my closest friends.'

That stung. But I told myself sternly that the feelings of hurt and exclusion that were my first reaction were out of all proportion to what he'd said, and I gave a mental shrug. If he wanted to act like a prima donna over his precious name, I thought defiantly, why should I care?

So I tilted my chin a little higher and rose to my feet.

'I see. Right,' I looked at my watch. 'Well, I must be going.'

It was completely untrue, I had nothing pressing to go home for, but the former cosiness had been broken and there didn't seem anything else to say. 'I'll let you know as soon as the photo's ready.'

I turned straight down the passage in search of the photographer Quinn had mentioned. There seemed no point in waiting. The name 'Eve' was tastefully painted over the door and the window was full of photographic studies that I looked over with a critical eye before going in.

But Quinn had been right. These were ultra-professional, and probably very expensive. But I wanted only the best, didn't I? The bell jangled as I opened the door, and I was soon explaining what I wanted to the friendly middle-aged woman behind the counter.

Almost a week passed, during which I did very little except for some walking and sketching while the weather held. I was feeling very solitary since Sue had left, and missed her lively company. Soon I would have to decide what I was going to do with the rest of my life, before I turned into some kind of recluse. I realised that subconsciously I'd been thinking that my future might have included Quinn in it; but as that was not to be, I seemed to be at a loose end with no clear purpose at all.

However, at last a phone call came from Eve to say that the photos were ready. She'd done several so I could choose the one I liked best and wanted enlarged.

And they were wonderful. I was amazed at how well they had turned out, given the unpromising, dirt-encrusted state of the painting.

'Oh, nowadays, computer enhancing can do marvels.' Eve smiled as I told her how surprised I was, then indicated the one I wanted her to enlarge.

'I'll have it ready for you by tomorrow afternoon,' she said with a smile as I left.

* * *

I phoned Quinn the following evening, using the number on his business card, as the studio would be closed by now. Knowing how keen he was to get working on the painting, I wanted to make sure he would be there in the morning when I took it round.

'Hi, Alex.' The familiar voice came over the line and I told him why I was calling.

'Oh, well, no. Actually, I shan't be at work tomorrow. I'm going up to Bristol for a couple of days.'

'What? I thought you couldn't wait to start on the picture.'

'Alex, I wouldn't choose this moment if it were up to me, but it's very important, and I have to go.' He paused. 'But you could drop the picture over here now, if you wouldn't mind. Would you do that? It's not very far to come, is it? Then I'll get to work on it as soon as I'm back. It'll be quite safe here until then.'

I gave a mental shrug. Obviously he wasn't going to expound. 'All right. I'll come right away.'

'Sure. See you in a minute.'

Quinn, I discovered, lived in a flat on the second floor of a converted fisherman's cottage overlooking the windy panorama of Porthmeor beach.

'Come on up,' he said as he opened the door to my knock. I followed him up the flight of stone steps and into a large airy room with a wide view of sea and sand.

'Oh, this is gorgeous,' I said, crossing to look out of the window. 'What a view!'

Quinn nodded. 'It's been converted from a former sail loft. I love it. The view is constantly changing with the weather and the tides.'

I turned into the room and sat down on the sagging but comfortable sofa, overlooking the beach.

'In winter, drifts of sand get blown up right over the doorstep, and really huge tides have been known to batter the house itself. We always keep a supply of sandbags on hand in case.' He pointed down to the concrete apron below. I stood up again and saw a couple of surfboards and a kayak propped against the wall, along with the sandbags he'd mentioned.

'Do you go surfing?' I asked. It didn't really fit the image of the quiet, intense man I knew him to be.

Quinn chuckled. 'Not me. They belong to the chap in the other flat. I like a swim as much as anybody, but that's enough. Sit down,' he added, 'I'll be right back.' He crossed the room and went into a kitchen area just across the passage.

While he was away I took a quick glance around the room, looking again for any evidence of female company. However, there was nothing remotely like it. A pile of picture frames was stashed in one corner and a couple of pairs of socks and a tea-towel were drying on the windowsill in the sun. There was a layer of dust on the shelf holding a pile of battered paperback books and a cracked mug full of pens and pencils

Quinn returned with a couple of mugs in his hand. 'Coffee,' he said simply. 'I was sure you could drink one, so I put the kettle on when I saw you coming up the road.'

'Oh, thanks, you're a mind-reader.' I smiled as I took it. 'What excellent service!'

'Better than any restaurant.' Quinn returned the smile as he sank down onto the sofa beside me. He cleared his throat and, looking down at his drink, said quietly,

'Alex, I asked you over for another reason, as well as for the picture. That was just an excuse. I didn't want to be interrupted like we might be in the shop.'

'Oh?' I turned my head swiftly.

'Yes. I think I owe you an apology.' He paused as I stared at his bent head. He was so close I could see the tiny pulse throbbing in his temple, and was very aware of the warmth of his body as our shoulders touched. He swirled his coffee round and watched as if fascinated by it. 'In fact, I know I do.'

I looked up in surprise. 'Apology? For what?'

'For the other day . . . when you asked me what my full name was. Do you remember?' Quinn raised his head and turned to look directly at me.

'Oh, er — yes, I do.' I stared at him. This was very unexpected.

'I snapped at you and I needn't have done. I must have sounded abrupt and rude. So, as I said, I'm really sorry if I hurt your feelings.'

I felt a little lift. So, he had noticed. And to have remembered it all this time, he must have realised my reaction. So he *was* the sensitive, caring person I'd taken him for. I looked into the steady brown eyes and something melted inside me. There were little flecks of gold in them picked up by the light, and his hair smelled of sea air and sunshine.

'Because,' he went on, 'friends shouldn't have secrets, and I'd like to think that we are . . . er . . . friends.' As his glance met mine over the top of his mug, and held, I swallowed hard and tore my gaze away as warmth flooded my face.

'I'd like that, too,' I said softly and took a sip of coffee to hide my flaming cheeks.

'So I want to tell you the whole story, to make amends.'

Quinn put aside his mug and looked down at his hands as he paused for a moment. Then he raised his head and gave a rueful smile. 'It's short for Quintinus.'

'For *what*?' I felt my eyes widen, and stifled a laugh, but he must have noticed.

'You see?' he said shortly. He spread his hands and shrugged. 'I'm one of five — I have two brothers and two sisters, all older than me. When I was born, my mother was reading those detective stories set in Roman times, and she came across the name there.'

His brows drew together. 'My parents thought it would be an appropriate name for their fifth child, never considering how that child might feel about it when he grew up. So,' he glowered, 'I'm Quintinus Nancarrow. But I never admit to it if I can help it. And, as I said, I only tell my closest friends.' He paused and as our eyes met and held their gaze, I felt a little bubble of warmth at the compliment. 'So now you know.'

The moment lasted until I felt I had to say something. 'Yes.' I nodded. 'And thank you for telling me, Quintinus.' Then we both burst out laughing.

After some small talk, I excused myself and went to the bathroom. Not so much because I needed the facilities — although I did — but if there was any female presence in the flat, it would surely be there.

But I drew a blank again. Stark and purely practical, there were no lotions, hand creams or scented soaps to give any indication that the place was other than what it seemed: a bachelor flat. And again, I wondered why not.

9

So Quinn was going to be off on his mysterious trip for a day or two. It must have been something very important to take him away now, as I knew how eager he was to get on with the work on my painting. But knowing he kept his private affairs very close to his chest, I hadn't expected him to tell me any details. Besides which, it was nothing to do with me.

Except that he still seemed to be getting under my skin more and more, however much I tried to ignore it. However sternly I told myself that he was a married man and would never be more than a friend, his face kept flitting into my head at odd moments when I hadn't been consciously thinking about him at all. When I was out sketching I could feel him looking critically over my shoulder; when I strolled around St.

Ives, his shadow would walk beside me; and his dark eyes haunted my dreams.

But lately, a new and less charitable thought had crossed my mind. What if he was being so friendly and stringing me along for a reason? The thought became an unpleasant possibility. Was Quinn actually as genuine and open as he appeared to be? Or was I being taken in by his magnetic charm? Was I failing to see what could be right under my nose because I was so strongly drawn to him?

Trying to ignore the personal side of our relationship for a moment, I took an unbiased look at the plain facts. One, I was the owner of a potentially valuable painting, wasn't I? Which would bring a great deal of publicity and prestige to the person who had discovered it and restored it to its original state. Quinn.

Two, I also possessed a highly desirable cottage in a location where house prices were astronomical. And three, I had been left a considerable legacy as well.

Even as I was turning all this over in my mind, though, I found it hard to believe. However, although I'd never in my wildest dreams thought of Quinn as a gold-digger, the evidence was there, wasn't it?

The very idea was anathema to me, but the more I thought about it the more possible it seemed, for how well did I actually know him? Only from my own impressions, and the purely physical effect of his personality.

I was totally confused. Every nerve ending I possessed was telling me to trust him, and I could usually rely on my instincts, but I had trusted Paul. And look where that had landed me.

However much I told myself that Quinn was different from Paul, there still remained that hurtful little niggle of doubt.

I spent a restless night filled with thoughts like these, and arose next morning unrefreshed and irritable. But today I would keep the promise I made to Granny Lou and Philippa, and go back to Lamorna to see them again. It would take my mind off the other things and give me something positive to do.

Only this time it wouldn't be such an easy journey. I had no car as yet, though I intended to get one now I had some money. So, I would go on the bus as far as it would take me, and walk the rest of the way if necessary. I enjoyed walking if I could stroll at my own pace, and stop and stare when I wanted to. Not like Sue's style of striding out at full tilt, her eyes always on the horizon, or around the next bend. Now, with all the time in the world to amble, I was looking forward to it.

I hadn't phoned Chycarn in advance, but if it was inconvenient to call on them, at least I would have had a pleasant day out. And, being a holiday complex, there was bound to be someone around.

I went in through the reception area and found Philippa busy making an elegant flower arrangement for the corner of the counter. She looked up as I entered and her face brightened.

'Alex! How lovely to see you.' She put down her scissors and wiped her hands on her apron.

'Hello, Pippa. I promised you both I'd come back for another visit, didn't I? So here I am.'

She came forward and gave me a hug. 'I hope it's a convenient time for you,' I said. 'If not, I can go for a stroll down to the cove and come back later.'

'It's perfectly fine. Gran's just woken up from her nap, so she'll be at her best now. Come on through.'

I followed as she bustled down the passage and this time led me straight into the kitchen, where Louisa was sitting by the window overlooking the garden, watching the birds coming and going around the feeders that were set up nearby.

She turned as we entered and her face creased into a welcoming smile. 'Alex, my dear!' She extended a hand. 'So you *did* come back. I'm so glad.'

I bent and clasped the gnarled fingers in mine. 'Hello, Granny Lou. Of course I did. I promised you, didn't I?'

'I'll make some tea,' said Philippa, 'and then I'll leave you two together. I've rather a lot to do.' At that moment the bell sounded in the reception, and I jumped up.

'Oh, let me make the tea, Pippa, shall I?'

'Oh, would you, dear? That would be wonderful.' She was taking off her apron as she spoke. 'Everything's to hand over there, and Gran can tell you if you can't find anything you need. That flowery cup and saucer is hers.'

I nodded and crossed the room to the working area. As I set out cups and waited for the kettle to boil, I took another look at the paintings hanging on the wall above. This time I was close enough to see the signature on them all.

On my first visit I had been so amazed by the discovery that the artist was there, right beside me, that I hadn't bothered to scrutinise them any further.

But now my heart skipped a beat as I stared at them, then stared again. For they were all signed 'L. Nicholson'.

I gasped and glanced at the bent old lady across the room. There *had* to be a connection. And I *had* to ask her what it was.

I carefully placed the fine bone china cup and saucer on the small table beside Louisa's chair, and smiled. No cheap and cheerful modern mugs for her, then, like the ones I was filling for Philippa and myself.

'I'll take Pippa's tea through to her and be right back,' I told the old lady as I left the room. There were people at the desk, so I placed the mug discreetly in a corner. Philippa gave me a grateful nod and smile.

'Granny Lou,' I said, pulling up a chair to sit beside her, 'there's something a bit personal I'd like to ask you, if you don't mind.'

She gave me her full attention, her bright eyes twinkling. 'Oh, that sounds ominous,' she said with a chuckle. 'I shan't know if I mind or not until you tell me what it is, will I?'

I perched on the edge of the seat where we could face each other. 'Well, I noticed your paintings are signed 'L. Nicholson'. Was that your maiden name?'

'Yes, dear, it was. Why do you ask?'

'Because,' I licked dry lips, 'there was a famous painter called Alfred Nicholson who was working around here at about the same time as you were a girl. He was a friend of Mr. Birch. And I just wondered ... I know it's not an uncommon name ... but were you related to him, by any chance?'

'Ah.' The smile slid from the old lady's face and she turned away to gaze out at the garden. A long pause followed, during which my heart started thumping and I felt my colour rise. Oh, whatever had I said? Had I upset her? But it was only a chance enquiry as far as she was concerned, she had no idea why I wanted to know. So ... why ... ?

At last she turned back to me with a

long sigh. 'Oh, it was all so long ago that it doesn't matter any more. I might as well tell you the whole story.'

'Are you sure?' I said anxiously, 'I don't want to pry if you'd rather not.'

She nodded. 'I'm sure. When you do get to my age, maid, nothing matters very much any more.' She took a sip of tea, returned the cup to its saucer with a shaking hand and cleared her throat.

'The fact is, Alex dear, Alfred Nicholson was my father.'

'Your *father*?' Amazement hit me like a physical blow as I felt my eyebrows shoot up to my hairline. 'But what . . . why . . . ?'

Louisa held up a hand. 'It's not as simple as it sounds. I was born, my dear, 'on the wrong side of the blanket', which is how they referred to it in my day.'

'The wrong . . . ' I frowned. Then the penny dropped. 'Oh, I *see*.' I gasped as the truth sank in. That's why she'd hesitated so before telling me. For to be illegitimate in her day was to be born

146

under a stigma so enormous it affected your whole life. I wondered how badly she had suffered as a young woman. And her mother even more so.

'So now you know.' She looked down at her lap and twisted her wedding band.

I reached out a hand and squeezed her fingers. 'Thank you so much for telling me.'

'Yes, he was a married man, but it made no difference,' Louisa went on dreamily, her gaze on the fluttering birds around the feeder. 'Such a romantic figure he was, one of these larger-than-life people, you know? Apparently he swept my mother quite off her feet. Strangers from 'up country' were a real rarity in this quiet corner of the world, you see.'

Her gaze met mine, and I saw that a haunting sadness had replaced her usual twinkle.

'The way he dressed, in colourful velvet suits and big floppy hats, he seemed to me as a small child like some

exotic creature from a foreign land.'
Louisa gave a wistful smile.

'I idolised him when I was a little
girl. I didn't know any of the
background, of course, and my mother
never told me anything. He set us up in
a little cottage not far from here. I
learned later that he had a wife in
London, who stayed there while he
came down to paint. He went to and
fro, but she was a city woman
apparently, and had no intention of
burying herself in a remote Cornish
hamlet. Whether she ever knew about
us, his other family, or not, I've no
idea.' She paused, lost in the past.

'Were . . . were you and your mother
cold-shouldered by the local people? Or
didn't it affect your lives too much?'
Still on the edge of my seat, I sat
spellbound by these ancient revelations.

'Well, my father lived with us against
all the rules of respectable society, but
there were a growing number of
bohemian types all around in those
days — artists, writers, poets — and I

don't think theirs was the only unusual relationship.' She shrugged. 'People tended to look upon them all like some kind of different species, and didn't expect them to behave normally.' She smiled and spread her hands.

'The happiest time of my childhood was when my father was with us. I trailed around behind him watching him painting, marvelling at the way he created beautiful pictures from the scenery around us, and I vowed I'd become a painter myself one day. When he saw how interested I was, he would sometimes give me a canvas that he wasn't pleased with, for me to paint over.' My heart lurched. Yes, it fitted.

Louisa's face crinkled in a smile of recollection. 'Alfred was a very temperamental person, you never knew what sort of mood he'd be in from one day to the next. If a work wasn't going well he'd paint it out in a temper and toss it over to me. I could never hope to be as good as he was, of course; but I enjoyed trying, as you can see.' She raised a hand to indicate the pictures around the room.

'You run yourself down, just like Pippa said.' I smiled at her. 'You were more talented than you gave yourself credit for.'

'I don't know about that, my handsome, but I dearly loved doing it.'

She sighed, back in the past again. 'Then in 1939, when war broke out, Father was called up and he went back to London for good. After that, it was as if a light had gone out in our house.' She sighed and her face grew sombre.

'Well, I grew up and went into service in a big house in Penzance, and became caught up in my new life, so I didn't miss him that much. But my mother was left alone, and now that Alfred was gone, she *was* shunned and treated badly by the locals. He broke her heart, I think. She never got over him and she died young.' Louisa's eyes were misty.

She dabbed at them, then straightened. 'As for me,' she said, taking in a deep breath, 'I married the first man that asked me, for the sake of respectability. He was a farm labourer, a good man, but with nothing in his head except his work. We rubbed along all right, but he could never understand why I was so taken up with painting. Waste of time, he called it. I should be doing something more useful.' She turned to me with a frown. 'Fred expected his wife to be in the kitchen, his home to be run like clockwork and all his meals on the dot.'

That touched a chord. It was something I knew about only too well, and I patted the old lady's hand in a gesture of sympathy, as her voice died away.

'So I put my paints away and closed the door on that chapter of my life. Then children came along, and my time was taken up in a very different way.' Louisa kept my hand in hers as she went on talking, more to herself than to me.

'But that was all so long ago, it's almost like a different lifetime.' She sighed and straightened. I shifted the cushion behind her back and she gave a grateful nod.

'I know at my age I can't have much time left to me, but I'm more content now than I've ever been. I'm very lucky, what with my son and daughter-in-law living here, and Pippa and her husband always about the place. I'm well looked after and I have plenty of company. Some of the visitors come and talk to me when they're staying here, and I meet a lot of interesting people.'

She turned to me and gently squeezed my fingers. 'And it's been lovely seeing you, my handsome.' As she gave a smile and removed her hand I could see her eyelids drooping, and realised how much these memories had taken out of her.

'I'm so sorry, I've tired you out, haven't I?' I said contritely, rising to my feet. 'But I'm so grateful to you for telling me all that, I really appreciate it.'

I dropped a brief kiss on her wrinkled

cheek. 'Goodbye, Granny Lou. Thank you so much for talking to me.'

She was asleep before I'd crossed the room.

10

I took a walk up to the craft studios a few days later, on the off-chance that Quinn might have returned, although I'd been expecting him to phone me when he had. But now, I was so eager to tell him what I had discovered at Lamorna that I couldn't keep away.

It was a cooler day, with a fine veil of cloud hiding the sun and turning the sea to a gauzy pearl grey. Rain coming in later, I thought.

To my surprise, Quinn's door was open and a radio was playing softly in the background. He looked up from the bench as I entered and broke into a broad smile.

'Alex! Good to see you.' He stopped what he was doing and came towards me.

'Hello, Quinn.' I smiled, but it was a bit frosty. I was irritated. Why couldn't he have let me know he was back? Then a small voice replied: Why should he? I acknowledged this was true. However, after his speech about us being 'friends', and also as I'd left the picture with him that he was so keen to start on, it wasn't too much to expect, surely?

But the broad smile of welcome was genuine, and as we met, Quinn extended a hand and seized mine, drawing me over to the workbench. The hand was warm and dry, and as he gave it a squeeze with his long, clever fingers, a jolt of electricity shot all the way up my arm. I suppressed a gasp of shock as he drew me behind the bench.

'I've started on this, look.' He dropped my hand as he pointed to the painting. 'I only got back last night, but I learnt so much I had to get on to it right away.'

He must have noticed my baffled expression as he paused and frowned. 'I did tell you I was going up to Bristol to that weekend workshop, didn't I?'

I shook my head. 'Actually, no, you didn't.' I smiled. So that was the mysterious business that I'd been wondering about. For, yes, I'd thought again that his wife might have been involved. Now I mentally scolded myself for being so nosy. But why *didn't* he think to tell me? If he would only open up a bit and tell me more about himself, I wouldn't have to leave his personal life to my imagination, or his motives towards me to supposition.

'Oh, I'm really sorry.' Quinn looked contrite. 'Yes, it was on modern methods of cleaning paintings. And there was one session devoted to canvases that have been over-painted.' He turned to me with a grin. 'It was exactly what we need, Alex, and I bought the materials while I was up there so I could get down to it right away.'

'That's wonderful. So what have you done so far?' I drew up a tall wooden stool and sat on it.

'Not a great deal, but I've removed

some of the old varnish on your picture. I don't know whether you'd noticed all the craquelure on it, but . . . '

'All the what?' Puzzled I wrinkled my nose and frowned.

'Oh, sorry.' Quinn smiled. 'It means tiny cracks in the varnish — like crocodile skin.'

'Oh, I see. Yes, I know what you mean.'

'Well, what you thought was dirt, Alex, was mostly old, yellow varnish that's gone brown with age.'

'Is it coming off all right?' I enquired anxiously.

'Oh, yes.' He nodded. 'No problem there. Look, I'll show you. Come round.'

The picture was propped up against a shelf in the workroom. 'It's only partly done, as you can see. But you can see how bright the original colours were.'

'Yes,' I said wistfully, biting my lip as I turned away and sat back on the stool again. I'd have dearly loved to save my original, but I'd made a promise, hadn't

I? And I would keep it.

'Anyway, I'll explain what happens next.' He took in a breath, as if ready to give a long lecture. But I couldn't wait any longer to tell him my news.

'Quinn,' I interrupted, to his obvious surprise, 'hang on a minute. I've got something sensational to tell you. And I shall burst if I have to keep it to myself any longer.'

He looked at me, startled, then laughed. 'Well, heaven forbid that you should burst. A bit messy, don't you think?' He propped one hip on the bench and folded his arms. 'OK. Fire away.'

'Idiot! Listen, this is serious. I went back to Lamorna because I promised them I would. And this time, I noticed Louisa's signature on her paintings.' I drew in a breath.

'Quinn, her maiden name was Nicholson.' I paused for effect.

I wasn't disappointed. Quinn straightened up and stared at me. '*Nicholson? But . . . how . . . ?*'

'She's his daughter. Alfred was her

father. He had a relationship with Louisa's mother, although he was a married man. And Louisa was the result. She told me all her life story. It was really interesting, even apart from discovering that.'

'Wow, but that's amazing! Incredible!' Quinn had begun to pace restlessly around the studio, waving his hands about as he tried to take it all in. He came back to my side and stroked his beard reflectively as a small silence fell. 'Hmm, that explains a lot, doesn't it?'

I nodded. 'Alfred taught her a bit about painting, apparently, and she told me he used to give her the canvases he'd finished with to practise on.' I shrugged and spread my hands.

'So, end of story. The mystery solved. I didn't tell her about Alfred's signature being underneath my picture, but I think we should take it to show her when you've finished, don't you?'

Quinn nodded, but I could see he wasn't really listening. He'd turned back to the picture and was staring at it as if wishing he could see right through the paint to the one beneath.

'It's going to be such a long job, though.' He sighed. 'I've got to be so careful not to damage the Nicholson.' He pointed to a row of bottles and jars nearby. 'This is all the stuff I brought back with me. Solvents, detergents, scrapers, brushes of different sizes — some stiff, some soft . . . cotton buds . . . special cloths . . . 'how-to' books . . . '

Solemn-faced, he turned towards me and took a deep breath. 'Alex, I've got *weeks* of finicky work here. Not only with cleaning off your picture — that's not quite so difficult — but I have to find out what pigment Nicholson used when he painted out his own. That is crucial, if I'm going to use the right stuff to remove it without spoiling the whole thing.'

'But I'm sure you can, and will.' I smiled at him.

'Huh! Your faith in me is very touching.' Quinn snorted.

I slid from the stool and paced the

studio, too restless to sit still. 'Oh, I'm longing to see what the subject of his painting was, and why he wasn't pleased with it, aren't you?'

'Of course I am,' Quinn said abruptly, only half-listening. I could see he was weighing up the task ahead, so I turned away.

'Well, I'll leave you in peace for a few days to get on with it. Let me know how it goes, and good luck.'

A grunt was his only reply.

★ ★ ★

So, while I was waiting for news of Quinn's progress, I occupied myself with doing up the cottage, both inside and out. Salt winds from the sea had been steadily eating into the paintwork during the time it had been standing empty. The interior had been kept clean and aired by the estate agents, but it hadn't been decorated for years.

I engaged a succession of builders to check the roof and the outside masonry, and painters to follow behind them. Indoors, I took up the old carpets and ordered new ones, along with fresh curtains to hang when the decorating had been done.

And all the while, my inner thoughts were of Quinn. I saw his familiar face, heard his voice, imagined his tender smile, in every move I made. My outer self could be busily chatting to the workmen, organised and completely on top of things, but my thoughts were drifting along completely different lines . . . Would he like this colour paint? These fabrics? What was his taste in furnishings? And, wistfully, how wonderful it would be if we were doing all this together, for a home of our own . . .

At last the whole house smelt sweet and clean. I took a long look around and felt a huge sense of satisfaction. I'd managed to keep the character of the old cottage along with the modern improvements, which was exactly what I'd been aiming at. The result was tasteful with a hint of understated elegance about it.

And I was amazed how many weeks had passed without me really noticing. Now I had time to myself again, I realised how long it had been since I'd had any contact with Quinn. Apart from a brief phone call when he'd said the work was going well, but slowly, I'd neither seen or heard anything of him. I resolved to go over to the studio right away.

*   *   *

We were into September by now, and with the children back at school, the summer visitors had thinned out and the town was a little quieter. A period of calm, mild weather had set in, and I stopped to lean on the railings overlooking the harbour, drinking in the fresh, salty air. It was a welcome relief from the smell of paint, which still lingered in the cottage despite all the windows being wide open.

Little sugar-pink clouds like candy

floss were drifting leisurely on a soft breeze, and there was hardly a ripple on the sea. A gaggle of gulls were fighting and screaming over some fish-heads being thrown overboard by a fisherman, and nearby a couple of oystercatchers were running along the tide edge on their little red legs, looking for their food too.

I straightened up as I remembered where I was supposed to be heading, and hurriedly turned round a sharp corner towards the studio.

Head down and not really looking where I was going, I was brought up short as I ran straight into a tall figure coming the other way.

'Oh! Oh, I'm *so* sorry . . . ' I gasped, as the man put both arms on my shoulders to steady me. 'Quinn! I was just coming round to see you . . . '

'Well, now you have. Oh, Alex!' Laughing, Quinn pulled me to him in a big hug, shaking his head at my foolishness. 'Don't you ever look where you're going? This is the second time

164

you've fallen into my arms, remember?'

'I know — on the train.' I smiled and felt myself flush. Then I realised Quinn was still holding me in the circle of his arms. The moment lengthened as neither of us moved. My treacherous heart had started pounding so rapidly I was sure he could feel it through the light top he was wearing. I was acutely aware that my face was pressed against the taut muscles of his chest, and that he seemed in no hurry to release me.

I thought I felt the touch of his cheek as it brushed against my hair, then I stiffened with shock as I realised. It wasn't his cheek, but his lips. He'd dropped a light kiss on the top of my head.

I raised my head to pull away but as our eyes met I was astonished at the expression on his face. Warm, tender, he was gazing down at me with a softness I'd never seen before, and for a second as his lips hovered above mine, I thought . . .

But no! This was a married man,

remember? And one whose integrity I wasn't sure about either. Especially if he was sending out the message he seemed to be, which meant he was also prepared to cheat on his wife.

'I understand,' I thought I heard him murmur as he straightened, 'it's too soon . . . '

It cost me more than Quinn would ever know, to pull away with some light remark and appear unfazed as I smoothed down my rumpled hair. I took in a deep breath. Nothing had outwardly changed, and the whole thing was over in seconds, but it seemed as if endless time had passed.

We fell into step and made small talk until we reached the studio. Then, as Quinn put the key in the lock and stood back for me to enter, I caught the excitement in his voice.

'Go through,' he said, and switched on the light in the inner room. 'There it is.' He waved a hand and followed me through.

'Oh! Oh, *Quinn*.' I squealed and

gasped in astonishment. 'Oh, my goodness — you've finished it!' My eyes widened as I took a step nearer.

There, propped on an easel and glowing with colour, stood the new painting.

11

I stepped forward, my heart pounding. 'It's *beautiful*,' I whispered in awe as I gazed and gazed at the scene.

Set in a leafy valley beside a trickling stream stood an old stone cottage, where in the open doorway a woman wearing a long white apron was holding a ginger cat in her arms. At her feet, chickens pecked in the grass, and a black-and-white collie dog was sitting in a slanting ray of sunshine, eyeing up a blackbird perched on the overhanging branch of an apple tree in full flower.

Under the tree stood a young girl in a pink dress, her blonde hair piled on top of her head, feathery tendrils framing her heart-shaped face. She was posing with a spray of apple blossom in one hand while the other rested on a low branch. It was a depiction of a rural idyll, set in quieter days and in an age long gone.

'What a wonderful job you've done.' I half-turned. 'Aren't you thrilled to bits with it?'

Quinn nodded with quiet pride. 'Read the caption,' he said briefly.

I hadn't noticed that, so intent was I on the picture itself. I bent my head and leaned forward. Then my heart missed a beat. ' 'Mary and Lou',' I read, ' 'Lamorna 1939'.'

I felt my jaw drop as my eyes met Quinn's. 'But that's *Granny* Lou! As a girl! She told me Alfred set her and her mother up in a cottage there. How fantastic!' I turned to Quinn and knew that my eyes were shining with delight.

'It is, isn't it? But I'm still wondering why Alfred painted it out and discarded it. I don't suppose we shall ever know that.' Quinn seemed deep in thought as he tapped his knuckles on the bench and gazed into space.

'Well, the date's 1939, the year war broke out. Louisa said he was called up then and went back to London. I don't think they ever saw him again.'

'Tell you what, though.' Quinn came out of his reverie and pulled out his laptop from a shelf below the bench. 'Let's look him up on Google. A famous person like him is sure to have an entry of some sort. Come round here.'

He made room for me to sit down, and leaned over my shoulder to tap in the query. I tried to ignore his warm breath on my neck and the faint, clean scent of peppermint about him. When a lock of his hair brushed my cheek I jumped as if stung, but he didn't seem to notice. I had to force myself to concentrate on the screen.

'Yes, here we are,' he said with a smile of satisfaction. 'Look, there's quite a long biography of the man.'

We scanned the pages together. *Alfred Nicholson, later 'Sir' Alfred, was a highly influential artist in the years between the two world wars. Himself a product of the Newlyn School, he spent much time in Cornwall, teaching and encouraging aspiring artists in the* school's distinctive genre of open-air studies.

'Yes. Well, we know all that,' Quinn muttered, scrolling down the article. 'Ah, this is more like it.'

Little is known of his private life. Although married, his wife Dorothy never, as far as we know, came to Cornwall, but remained at their home in London. There were rumours that he had a liaison with a local girl, some say resulting in a child, although this was never proven.

Upon the outbreak of war, he was recalled to London and joined the army, to be captured by the Japanese three years later and interned for the duration. After his release Nicholson became a changed man, his experiences having left him scarred forever. His paintings undertook a drastic change at this point, becoming stark and grim. Gone were the rural scenes of happier times in Cornwall. This later work verges on the abstract. There is a notable absence of colour in these scenes of brooding dark skies under which skeletal figures blur into the background of leafless trees and menacing black hills.

This complete change of style leaves a notable gap in his acclaimed series of the six 'Lamorna' paintings, one of which is missing and has never been traced. Fellow artists believe he destroyed it in frustration at having to tear himself away from Cornwall to go to war.

For further reading, the following books are recommended . . .

'And that seems to be it.' Quinn closed down the laptop and turned to face me. 'So Alex, you do see how vitally important this is, don't you?' He indicated the painting beside us.

I nodded and swallowed hard. 'So, what do we do next?' I said in a small voice.

'I need to talk to some contacts I still have in the art world, in London.'

'How do you mean, you 'still have' contacts? Have you spent much time in London?'

'Er . . . ' Quinn turned his back and

took more time than he needed to put the laptop away. 'Um, yes, actually. It's where I did my training in art restoration.'

His gaze remained fixed on the view outside. It left me with the impression that there was a lot more he could have said, but obviously wasn't going to.

I gave him time, but as the pause lengthened, I said, 'But before you speak to your London contacts, there's something I think we should do.'

'Oh?' He raised an eyebrow. 'What's that?'

'I want to go to Lamorna again, and show the painting to Granny Lou.'

'Ah, yes. Yes, you did mention that. OK, we will. I'll come with you. I'd like to meet the old lady. She sounds quite a character. She might even remember her father painting it.' Quinn uncurled his long legs and stood up.

'Oh! I've just thought of something, though.' I jumped to my feet as well.

'What's that?' Quinn's head turned quickly as he looked at me, startled.

'A snag.' I nibbled my bottom lip. 'Quinn, how are we going to tell her we've destroyed *her* painting to reveal the Nicholson?'

'Hah, good question.' He frowned as our eyes met, both of us deep in thought.

'But we *don't* have to tell her, do we?' I felt my face brighten as I answered myself. 'Think about it. It could be a totally different picture. You're an art restorer. Someone brought it into the shop to be cleaned. Perfect truth. We just don't say it was me.' I turned on a heel and spread my hands wide.

'Yes.' Quinn nodded. 'That'll work. And if her father had painted it out before he gave the canvas to her, as she told you he used to, she won't know it was underneath her own picture anyway.'

'Phew!' We both laughed together and in the exhilaration of the moment, Quinn threw one arm around my shoulders and drew me to him in a warm half-hug. I immediately stiffened and drew away. But not before I'd caught an expression in his eyes of . . . what? Hurt? Disappointment?

He recovered in a second and flashed me a smile — which seemed to me, with my heightened sensitivity, to be a little strained.

'Oh, Alex, isn't it *exciting*!' he exclaimed heartily, as I nodded agreement and left.

★　★　★

So, back we went, on Quinn's next free day. Autumn was tinting the field hedges now, with the rust of bracken and the gold of the gorse bushes which never really stopped flowering. 'Kissing's out of favour when the gorse is out of bloom.' The old saying sprang to my mind, and I glanced involuntarily at the familiar profile beside me. If only . . . Well, I could dream, couldn't I? As long as I never lost my self-control and gave away by word or gesture the slightest hint of my feelings.

But thoughts like that would get me

nowhere. I fixed my gaze on the distant sea and made some unmemorable small talk to fill the silence that had fallen.

I'd phoned Philippa before we set out to make sure it was convenient to call, and let her know that I was bringing a friend with me.

'Yes, that'll be fine,' she said. 'Although Granny gets very tired these days, she'll be delighted to see you.'

It was a veiled hint that we should not stay very long. I'd already told Quinn this so he could be prepared, and not think he wasn't welcome. I'd become to feel so comfortable with these people that I almost thought of them as my own family, and Louisa as a kind of surrogate great-grandmother.

'Come through.' Philippa rose from her seat in reception. Her eyebrows lifted as I introduced Quinn. She'd obviously thought my 'friend' was going to be another woman.

'Granny's lying down today,' she said as she led us down the passage. 'On the day-bed. She was very pleased to hear you were coming. She doesn't see many people apart from us and some of our guests, and the days are long for her.'

The old lady was reclining on a couch in her favourite position overlooking the garden, propped up on several pillows. Her welcoming smile was as warm as ever as she reached out a hand and clasped mine. I leaned the picture carefully against the side of the bed as I bent to drop a kiss on the weathered cheek and turned to introduce Quinn.

She kept his hand in hers as she looked him carefully up and down. 'Sit down, both of you,' she said, indicating the cane chairs in the bay window.

'We've brought something to show you,' I said, perching on the edge of the chair as Quinn passed me the painting.

'Oh, another painting, is it?' She leaned forward eagerly as we unwrapped it together.

'What do you think of this, then?' Quinn said, with a gentle smile. 'Do you recognise anyone in it?'

She stared for a long moment at the

painted figures, her brow creasing as she took it in. Then: 'Well, bless my soul! It's . . . isn't it . . . ?' she muttered, then caught sight of the caption.

'Mary and Lou! Oh, my goodness. That's . . . that's . . . Mam and me!' She looked up at us, tears misting her eyes. 'Oh, my dears, wherever did this come from? I've never seen it before.' Quinn's eyes met mine and we exchanged a look of relief. That was our most awkward question answered. Louisa didn't wait for an answer to her own, but was peering closely at the date.

'That's 1939, is it?'

I nodded.

'Yes. I would have been twenty then. And that was the year my father went away. I remember posing for it. And Mother was annoyed to be dragged out of the kitchen because she was busy cleaning. But she would never refuse my father anything. I never saw him again, you know.'

There was a sadness in her tone. 'But — ' She turned her full attention on us. ' — how *you* come to have it, I can't possibly imagine.'

Between us, we launched into the story of its recovery. As she listened without interruption, I guessed she was tiring, and noticed that the painting was drooping in her hands.

So, as Quinn gently took it from her, I produced my trump card. I'd had Eve take a photo of the painting as she'd done for mine, and put it in a tasteful frame.

'This is for you to keep, Granny Lou,' I said.

This time tears trickled in earnest down her wrinkled cheeks. 'Oh, my dears, my dears, you'll never know what this means to me. Thank you *so* much.' She looked up at us and gave a wobbly smile. 'What a lovely young couple you are.'

She turned to Quinn and grasped his hand as she murmured, 'Look after her, my handsome, you've got a good little girl there. And I hope you'll be really happy together.'

I could hardly bring myself to look at Quinn. He'd had gone deep red and I knew I must be blushing too, from the sudden warmth in my cheeks.

'Oh, oh, no, Granny Lou! Quinn isn't . . . we're not . . . ' I babbled away in embarrassment. But the old lady was half-asleep, her eyelids drooping.

'The most important thing . . . never keep secrets from each other.' Her head was nodding. 'Share everything, good and bad. And always, always, settle your differences before the sun sets on them . . . ' Her voice trailed away into a gentle snore.

12

I couldn't look at Quinn as we went back through the house, said our good-byes to Philippa, and made our way outside to the car.

'What a remarkable old lady,' he said at last, as we settled ourselves before driving off. Then he turned to face me and added, 'But she did get hold of the wrong end of the stick, didn't she?' I expected him to break into a laugh as he spoke, or at least a smile, but his gaze was serious as he paused, obviously expecting a reply from me.

The moment lengthened as I struggled hopelessly to find an answer. Struggled, too, to break away from that penetrating look, and what it was doing to my composure.

Of course I longed to say that no, on the contrary, she'd been perfectly right; but that was naturally out of the question. I swallowed hard and balled my hands into fists until they hurt, then deliberately turned away to wave at Philippa behind us on the steps.

Then I casually glanced at my watch and deflected the mood with a trivial remark. 'Oh, a natural mistake, I suppose.' I shrugged and smiled.

I felt, rather than saw, Quinn give me another long look, before he started the engine and the moment passed.

★   ★   ★

'I have to go up to London on some business soon,' Quinn said as we were drawing into St. Ives.

We had stopped at traffic lights and he was tapping a hand on the wheel. Half-turning to me as he kept an eye on the lights, he said, 'I was wondering whether you'd mind, Alex, if I took the painting with me.' I raised an eyebrow.

'I need to show it to people in the art world — break the news of our amazing discovery.' His face was full of excitement, eyes sparkling as they met mine.

I sighed and shrugged. It had to happen, of course, I'd known that all along.

I suppose Quinn must have noticed my lack of enthusiasm, for he added, as if he was doing me a favour, 'I could maybe get it valued for you too, as you'll need to insure it, of course. What do you think?'

'I suppose so,' I said with reluctance. 'Then the great publicity machine will start rolling, won't it?'

'I'm afraid so. I know how you feel about that, but you did know this would happen.'

I nodded. I couldn't really explain my inner feelings to him, I could hardly put my finger on them for myself. I only felt that once the great news was made public, the painting would cease to be mine and Quinn's shared secret. And that I was about to lose a little of him along with it.

His gaze was still on my downcast face. 'Alex, you did promise, remember?' Now there was the slightest note of irritation in his voice.

'Yes,' I said with a sigh as the lights changed and we moved off. 'I did.'

I would like him to have told me what his other 'business' was in London, but I could hardly ask him outright.

However, I didn't have to. As if he had read my thoughts, Quinn muttered to himself, looking over his shoulder as he pulled out into the stream of traffic. 'I've got to meet Caroline at her office. She's been in the States working for a few months. We've got stuff to sort out. So it'll all fit in very nicely if I take the picture up with me as well.'

My heart plummeted. So *that* was why there had been no sight or sign of his wife all this time. And I'd begun to hope . . . or rather to dream . . . of how different things might have been . . . Stupid, really. I took in a deep breath, squared my shoulders, and pasted a smile on my face as I made some trivial reply.

★ ★ ★

184

Quinn left for the city the following week. 'I'll phone and keep you in touch,' he said breezily as he called round on his way, collected the painting and stowed it carefully in the car.

Then he was gone and the painting with him. After all the excitement we'd had over it, and how close we'd become, now the whole thing was on hold and Quinn lost to me, I found myself drifting idly about, not able to settle to anything.

I filled the gap by catching up on a backlog of correspondence from family and friends. Then, among the mixed bag of emails that I hadn't attended to for weeks, I came across one from my sister in Scotland, gently reminding me that our parents' ruby wedding anniversary was coming up.

We'd never been close as children, Julia and I. She was seven years older than me and too fond of ordering me around. After she married and went to live in Aberdeen we'd seen little of each other, except for family occasions like this one.

I gathered that Julia had more or less arranged the whole thing already. She was a great organiser and thoroughly enjoyed doing it, which I wouldn't have. So I let her get on with it and told her I would just show up on the day.

The day before I was due to leave, however, I was not feeling at all well, with a sore throat and tickly cough hinting at a cold to come. Not welcome at the best of times, but even less so in the summer months and with a special occasion in front of me. One that I could not easily get out of, and didn't really want to — I hadn't seen my family for about a year and my conscience had been pricking me lately. When this came up I'd hailed it as an ideal solution.

But I didn't want to be sneezing and blowing over everyone at the party, so I packed every remedy I could think of to take with me, and dosed myself well when I went to bed.

I awoke next morning with a splitting headache to add to the cough, but

— doggedly telling myself it would wear off during the day — I swallowed down some ibuprofen for breakfast and dragged myself up the steep hill to the station. After changing at St. Erth I'd be able to settle back and relax for the rest of the way to Plymouth.

I must have dozed off for most of the journey, for when I opened my eyes next, we were crossing Brunel's great bridge across the Tamar, out of Cornwall and into Devon.

My parents' house was within walking distance from the station, set in a pleasant, leafy cul-de-sac. As my bag was quite light, I set off, telling myself the air would do me good. To a certain extent it did, and meeting the family would take my mind temporarily off how I was feeling.

* * *

'Hello darling, you're looking well.'

'Hello, Mum, so are you. It's good to see you.' She was obviously attributing my heightened colour to all the wrong reasons. But then, Mum had always been the least observant of people. Usually lost in a world of her own, she floated through life with a vague and otherworldly air about her.

Her greatest love was music, which she had always taught. My childhood memories were of a string of strange children coming and going to her studio and hammering away at the piano.

Wearing a loose top of printed chiffon over slim black trousers, her still-dark hair swept into a knot on top of her head, my mother looked younger than her years. We exchanged air-kisses and I followed her into the house.

In contrast, my father welcomed me with a bear hug, then held me at arm's length while he looked me anxiously up and down.

'Are you quite well, Alex my dear?' he asked, pushing his spectacles further up his nose as was his usual habit.

I smiled into his sharp blue eyes. 'A

bit of a cold, Dad, that's all. I don't think I shall quite need a bell and a placard saying 'Unclean',' I joked, 'but I will keep my distance from everybody. Including you.' I smiled and took a step back.

We laughed together. 'Come through,' he said. 'Julia and the others are here.' I didn't need to be told, I could already hear the racket the children were making. I left my holdall in the hall and followed him into the sitting room.

My sister and her husband Ian, with their two young sons of five and three, were giving a rousing rendition of 'The Wheels on the Bus', which did nothing for my aching head. But I pasted a smile on my face and made an effort to be pleasant.

'Alex!' Julia removed the younger boy from her lap and stood up to greet me. 'What a long time it's been. How are you? Actually, you're looking a bit rough, if I may say so. Cornwall not agreeing with you?' We touched cheeks. Julia had never been the soul of tact. As a child she had been blunt in the extreme, always saying exactly what she felt, which had led to endless friction between us, and had not changed over time.

'Just a cold. I'll survive,' I smiled, 'and Cornwall is wonderful, I've never regretted the move. Hello Ian.' I raised a hand to him, then bent down to the little boys. 'Hello Max, Robbie; do you remember your Aunty Alex?'

Two blank little faces looked back at me and I realised with a stab of guilt that the gap had been too long for the children's memories.

'I hope you won't pass that cold on to them,' Julia remarked. 'They've only just got over chicken pox.'

Feeling like some kind of pariah, I rose to my feet, just as Mum came in with a tray of tea. At last I could sink into a deep armchair and relax.

'So where's the party being held?' I gratefully accepted a cup of tea, ambrosia to my sore throat.

'I've booked a room at the Royal Oak just down the road.' Julia raised a hand.

'For lunch, so the boys can come too.'

Mum was nodding her head in agreement. 'Of course they must come.'

Behind her, Ian was draining his tea as he glanced at his watch. 'Don't forget the time, darling,' he broke in. 'Remember, we promised the boys . . . '

'Oh, yes, of course. Sorry to dive off so soon, Alex, but we were just going. We're taking Max and Robbie up to a funfair on the Hoe on the way back to the hotel. They spotted it on the way down. But we'll see you again tomorrow. Bye Mum, Dad.'

Peace fell with their departure. Mum came drifting back from waving them off with a dreamy smile on her face. 'What a lovely little family they are,' she remarked, resuming her seat and picking up her cup again.

Turning to me she raised an eyebrow. 'And how are you finding the single life, Alex?'

'I'm loving it,' I said, meeting her eye. 'I wouldn't change a thing.'

'What a pity that you didn't stick

with Paul. Such a nice young man, I always thought. I just can't understand you.'

'You know nothing of what went on between us, Mum,' I said, just managing not to snap at her. 'We should never have married, we were like chalk and cheese.' I didn't add that I had expected the love and attention from him that I had lacked in my childhood.

'If you'd only had children it might have lasted. I always think that children cement a marriage. Look at Julia, now . . . '

Refusing to rise to it, I closed my ears and let it wash over me. It was a reminder of why I had left home in the beginning, and married the first man that asked me. Like a comfort blanket, I conjured up a picture of St. Ives — and consequently, Quinn — to calm my ragged nerves, and told myself that by this time tomorrow I'd be back there, duty done and conscience clear.

★ ★ ★

After a good night's sleep, next morning I was feeling a good deal better. However, I came downstairs to find my mother sitting over the breakfast table with one hand to her head, holding a hanky to her nose.

'Mum, what's the matter?' I asked in concern.

She gave me a venomous look. 'I've only caught your cold, thank you very much.'

'But that's ridiculous, you can't have done; colds take days to develop.'

'That's what I told her.' My father raised his brows and shrugged. 'But she won't listen.'

'Colds can come from anywhere; it must be a different strain.' Refusing to feel guilty or responsible, I gave her the remedies I'd brought with me, and by the time of the party she was a lot better. Well enough, in fact, to tell everybody how I'd brought the infection up with me.

I stayed long enough to eat lunch and greet all the relations I hadn't seen for so long; then, as soon as I decently could, I excused myself and caught the next train home. Home! How marvellous to be on my own again.

★ ★ ★

This diversion had taken my mind off Quinn and the painting, and by the time I returned from Devon I was hoping eagerly for a message from him.

There was one on the answerphone, along with several others, mostly from reporters practically queuing up to interview me for the papers, radio, TV. You name it, they were there. Quinn had obviously been successfully spreading the word while I'd been away. I ignored them all, put them on 'save', and keyed in to what he had to say.

'Alex, where on earth *are* you?' came his irritated recorded voice. 'I've been trying to get hold of you for *ages*. Phone me as soon as you can. I've got so much to tell you.' So that evening I called Quinn on his mobile and he answered right away.

'Alex! At last. Where've you *been*?' he said again. I started to tell him, but I could tell he wasn't really listening, just answering in monosyllables or grunts. Then he cut in as soon as I was finished.

'Well, I'll tell you this — your painting has caused a huge sensation. It's sent ripples through the whole art world. One of the major Bond Street galleries is practically begging to put it in an exhibition they've got coming up, but I said I would have to ask you first. So I had to give them your name. I'm sorry about that. I expect you've had reporters chasing you up by now. But you will let them, won't you? Exhibit, I mean.'

He paused to draw breath.

'I'll think about it,' I said guardedly.

'Well, don't take too long about it,' came the acerbic voice down the line. 'And Alex, because it's so precious, I've already had it valued, and you must take out insurance immediately.'

I was becoming increasingly irritated at Quinn's lecturing tone, but told myself that it was only because he was so excited. And under pressure of course, from the gallery owners. And he was doing the best he could for me.

Then he named a sum that nearly took my breath away. '*That* much?' My voice rose up the scale. 'Oh, I see what you mean.'

'Would you like me to see to that for you?' Quinn said eagerly. 'There's no time to lose, Alex, believe me. Once the word spreads, the painting could be wide open to danger from theft, fire, flood, defacement, anything . . . ' I couldn't resist a smile as I pictured him quite clearly. He would have his shoulders raised, hands spread, that curly forelock dipping into his eyes . . . Unexpectedly, I felt a lump in my throat. Oh, *Quinn*!

'Yes, if you will.' I was still irritated at the way he was taking over, but told myself again it was all for my benefit after all, and that he was absolutely right in his reasoning.

'And you will let them put it in the exhibition, won't you? It opens in a week's time. You must look in the papers for the reviews after that.'

'All right,' I grudgingly conceded. 'But Quinn, you must make it quite clear that it is absolutely not for sale.' I managed to assert myself at last. Up to now I'd been so bowled over by all he'd been telling me, I hadn't had a chance to think straight. Now I raised my voice. 'No way, under any circumstances whatsoever. Have you got that?'

'Wha . . . *what*? You're never going to *keep* it, surely? When it's worth all that money? You're out of your mind, Alex.' I could almost feel him bristling with indignation. 'You are *so* naïve. You'd have to put it in a bank vault for safekeeping, you know. You're not seriously thinking of hanging it on the wall like the old one, are you?' A sardonic snort came over the line.

At this point I'd had enough.

'Quinn,' I said through gritted teeth,

quietly and firmly, in contrast to his indignant raised voice, 'I'm grateful for what you've done in restoring that painting, and putting it in its rightful place as the lost Nicholson. But I'd like to remind you that it does belong to *me*, and that I shall do what I like with it.' I was annoyed to find I was actually shaking now, and hated myself for it.

'I don't like being told I'm some kind of idiot,' I continued. 'I have my own plans for that painting, and they don't include either keeping it or selling it to the highest bidder.'

'Then . . . then — what . . . ?'

'That's my business.' I was shouting now. 'And I'll tell you when you bring it back to me.' I slammed the phone down and burst into tears. It was a welcome release from a backlog of pent-up stress and frustration.

★ ★ ★

After I'd mopped myself up and calmed down once more, I scrolled through my messages again, ignoring the ones from the media, and found one from Sue that had just come in. It was brief and to the point.

'Alex, please, please phone me as soon as you can,' came the excited voice, 'I've got some great news to tell you.'

Intrigued, I dialled her number straight away.

After an introductory chat and catch-up, Sue obviously couldn't contain herself any longer. 'Alex, you know I said I had some great news to tell you, remember?'

'Of course I remember! I thought you were never going to get around to it,' I chuckled.

'Oh, you . . . Well, you might find this comes as a surprise, knowing me, but — ' She took in a breath. 'John has asked me to marry him — and I've said I will!'

'Oh, Sue, that is *fantastic*! I'm so pleased for you. For you both. I hope you'll be really happy together. John's such a nice guy.' I couldn't resist adding, 'So he wasn't just another 'pebble on the beach', then?'

Her tinkling laugh floated down the line. 'No, Alex, this is the real thing. I can tell. And what I want to ask you as well, is this.' She paused and cleared her throat.

'We're having a party to celebrate our engagement. And as my oldest friend, I'd dearly, dearly like you to come. Do you think you could? You don't have many commitments now, do you? You could stay with me, we could have a few days together first, so do say yes. It would mean so much to me.'

'In that case, how could I refuse?' I smiled broadly, forgetting that she couldn't see it, and thought — not for the first time — how limited a phone conversation is, and how frustrating it can be when you can't see the expression on the other person's face.

And no, I didn't have any commitments, I thought bleakly. She was absolutely right there.

'Yes, of course I'll come,' I went on. 'Wouldn't miss it for the world.'

A squeal of delight came from the other end and we spent the rest of the time making practical arrangements for the where, when and how of it all.

* * *

When we at last rang off, I began to consider what I should take with me in the way of clothes. Something smart for the party, of course, and other casual stuff for sightseeing and general purposes. Fortunately, I'd bought a new skirt when I was in Plymouth for the ruby anniversary party, which would come in very handy again. I would throw in my French navy trouser suit, the only other smart outfit I possessed, in case we went out to an upmarket restaurant. I didn't know Sue's habits in that way, so I would go prepared. Together with a few serviceable tops and a couple of pairs of trousers for everyday wear, that should be it.

I actually began to feel quite excited as I started to pack. It would take me far away from St. Ives, where I was constantly tormented by thoughts of Quinn and of what might have been.

13

Sue lived in an attractive ground-floor flat, part of an old Victorian house, set in a leafy avenue lined with large, stately trees.

'Oh, this is nice,' I remarked, looking around as we were getting out of the car. 'I didn't think it would be quite so rural-looking.'

'Yes. It's lovely, but still with the town not far away.' She opened the boot and handed me my bag. 'There was an old manor house near here once. This was part of the grounds, I think. There's actually a field up there, and a little bit of woodland.' She pointed with her free hand as she locked the car, and kept the hand poised long enough for me to realise she was flashing her fourth finger around in the air.

'Oh, *Sue*, what a lovely ring!' I caught hold of the hand to examine it more closely. A dainty sapphire flower sat in a circle of beaten silver.

She nodded happily. 'John chose it. He said because it matches my eyes. He said, too, I could change it if I wanted. But I don't. I just love it.' And her eyes were shining with a sparkle to equal that of the gem as she twisted it on her finger.

'Wonderful.' I couldn't resist a stab of — not envy, exactly, but an inner feeling of regret that I hadn't been as lucky as her in my choice of partner. Actually, I rarely thought of Paul nowadays, and sometimes couldn't even remember what he looked like.

'So when's the party?' I asked later as we were sitting over the remains of a meal. From the window we could look out over a green space beside a lovely old church that stood amidst patches of flowers and a few graceful trees.

'Saturday evening. The day after tomorrow.' Sue spoke over her shoulder as she picked up the empty plates and moved through to the kitchen.

'Right. You're not having it here, are you?' I looked around at the limited space in the flat.

'Goodness, no. I've booked a private room down at the pub. I don't really know how many are coming. It's been difficult to pin people down, so it's just open house really, with a running buffet.'

'Good.' I nodded. 'I'm really looking forward to it.' And I was. It seemed a long time since I'd had any fun. This was a complete change of scenery, it had taken me out of my own concerns for a day or two, and I was determined to enjoy myself.

'So, when's the wedding?' I asked Sue when she came back. 'Have you fixed a date for it yet?'

'Only provisionally.' She flopped into an easy chair. 'We thought in the spring, April or May perhaps. That'll give us a few months to make arrangements, put both our flats on the market, hopefully find a house . . . Alex, there is so much to think about.'

Wriggling in her seat, eyes sparkling with excitement, Sue looked like a child who'd been promised a visit to Disneyland. I couldn't help but compare our different situations, and turned away as I felt the smile suddenly slip from my face.

★　★　★

We had cleared away and were relaxing over our coffee, feet up in the sitting room, when I picked up the daily paper that Sue had finished with. And there it was, in letters seeming ten feet tall, leaping out at me. Far from what I'd thought, I *hadn't* left my other life behind after all.

It was headed 'The Lookout Gallery, Cork Street'. The article went on to say: *We are proud to announce a major exhibition by artists of the Newlyn School of painters, the largest collection we have ever shown by artists of this genre. We are particularly grateful to the owners of the paintings who have* generously *loaned them for this occasion.*

This event will also include the discovery of the century, the long-lost sixth painting in the series of 'Lamorna' works by Sir Alfred Nicholson. This was known to exist, but has never before been exhibited, having mysteriously vanished after the artist returned to London at the outbreak of the Second World War.

There followed details of dates and times.

'Wow!' said Sue as I passed it over to her. 'Alex, you just *have* to go to that.' She looked up and gave me a mischievous grin. 'Imagine the scene you'll cause when you tell them that it belongs to you!'

'Actually, I'd rather remain incognito,' I replied. 'I shall do my best to be invisible. It was Quinn who was so set on showing it. He said I owed it to the art world, or something.'

'Well, so you do, if it's as important as that.' Sue nibbled a lip. 'Actually, that's come up just at the right time. I've had a call from work asking if I could go in tomorrow and cover for someone who's sick. I told them I would only if it was urgent and they couldn't find anyone else to do it, because you were coming. But,' she said as our eyes met, 'if you've got this exhibition to go to, I shan't feel so guilty about leaving you on your own.'

'Oh, Sue, no, you mustn't feel like that! Even if this hadn't come up, I could have found somewhere to go. The last thing I want is to put you out at all. We shall have other days we can spend together.'

'Well, if you're sure, I'll phone and tell them I will come in, then.'

* * *

So the following afternoon I took a tube to the West End and walked through the fashionable streets to the gallery. Having become accustomed to life in St. Ives I was overwhelmed at the bustle of the city. I'd been used for so long to the immensity of the sea and skies of Cornwall, that the small amount of sky that was visible above the enormously high buildings seemed to be blotted out and diminished by them. Expensive cars whooshed past, taxis wove in and out of the traffic seeming to just avoid collision at every corner, while cyclists took their lives in their hands. People, too, all seemed to be in such a hurry, striding past as if on some urgent and important business. And of course, never a familiar face to be seen on these streets.

The gallery turned out to be an imposing building with two arched entrances and an impressive flight of marble stairs leading to the upper floor.

There were more people viewing than I had anticipated. Obviously the exhibition had generated a lot of interest. I walked past the walls lined with paintings by artists whose names had become so familiar to me. Here was Samuel — alias Lamorna — Birch,

Stanhope and Elizabeth Forbes, Laura Knight, and others.

Then, on a far wall, grouped together under soft lighting, were the works of the star of the exhibition, Sir Alfred Nicholson. My heart did a little flutter as I drew closer, and there it was. My own familiar 'Mary and Lou'. A lump came to my throat as I thought how wonderful it would be if Granny Lou could have seen this for herself.

The picture looked totally different in this setting — and, to my critical eyes, slightly diminished now it was only one among the rest of the series.

I spent some time going round the huge room and also listening to the comments of other viewers, mostly favourable, as they paused in front of the Nicholson.

I'd moved on when a woman's voice, louder than the rest, caught my attention. 'Of course,' she said, 'it was Quinn Nancarrow who discovered that lost painting, you know.'

My heart gave a lurch and I froze,

not daring to turn round and stare. Seemingly transfixed by the nearest picture, I gazed unseeingly at it and listened hard.

'Nancarrow?' replied her male companion. 'Do I know him?'

'Don't you remember, darling? He used to work here. Tall, thin, dark; rather nice-looking, actually, with a bit of a beard. You *must* remember him — he was very clever and highly thought of as a restorer. Then he had a breakdown and there were lots of problems. Personal ones too, I think. He married Caroline Bond, you know? Press secretary here. I knew her slightly.'

The languid voice paused, presumably to look at one of the exhibits, and the man replied: 'Oh, *him*. Yes, vaguely — look, isn't this one marvellous, darling? See the contrast in the light and that shading? Masterly.'

'Mm, lovely. Afterwards, he disappeared back down to Cornwall where he came from to recover, and never came back. I believe he became more or less a recluse. Such a waste of talent.'

The voices faded as the couple moved on, and whatever else was said was lost in the hum of the crowd. I turned to see who the two were, but a bunch of schoolchildren were coming in and the couple were nowhere to be seen.

I stumbled limply to a bench and sat down to rest my shaking legs. Well! So Quinn had had a breakdown at some time. Maybe that was why he was so reluctant to open up about himself. And he'd never mentioned how skilled he'd been before that.

My thoughts ran on. When he'd started on my Nicholson, he'd been so hesitant about whether he could do it, I had no idea he'd once been such a professional. But if the breakdown he'd suffered had robbed him of his confidence, that could have been the reason.

I was walking back, still deep in thoughts of Quinn when, coming to a couple of offices situated on a bend in the stairs, I saw a woman just coming out of one, speaking on a mobile phone. As I passed, I couldn't help but overhear a snatch of her conversation as she was ringing off.

'. . . OK. I'll be seeing Quinn later, that's fine. I'll tell him then.'

I almost tripped over the next step and had to grab the handrail to steady myself. Had I really heard that, or was it only because he was in my head at the time?

I soon found out. As the woman came hurrying down the stairs and passed me, a young man with a sheaf of papers under his arm called after her from the office doorway.

'Caroline — can you spare a moment? Shan't keep you long, it's just about this . . . ' The rest of the sentence was lost as the gaggle of schoolchildren began to leave the gallery.

She turned with a smile. 'Of course you can, darling,' she replied, retracing her steps up the stairs. As I paused to let the children go by I took a good look at Caroline. Hers was a fairly common name, but coupled with that of 'Quinn', which certainly wasn't, it couldn't be dismissed as mere coincidence. Besides, hadn't the woman in the gallery said Caroline worked here? Pretty conclusive, then.

She was tall and slender, with bottle-blonde hair piled in an untidy heap on top of her head and fastened with a butterfly clip. Heavily made up and wearing a tight black skirt and four inch heels, she was the last person I would have associated with Quinn.

But there it was: this was his wife and they were obviously still close. I sighed, swallowed hard and went on my way.

I crossed the road and strolled aimlessly, trying to sort out my teeming thoughts. I had no idea how far I had walked, but when I came back to the present I found myself entering a park and sat down gratefully on the nearest bench to rest my aching legs.

We were nearly into October now,

and a thin and penetrating easterly wind was bending the branches of the stately trees. It was chilly, not weather to be hanging around in. I hunched myself further into my collar, thrust both hands into my coat pockets and moved on. A few dry leaves were being tossed around among the bits of paper and other litter that swirled around my feet. Summer was over, and with it my hopes and dreams. I swallowed down the lump in my throat and headed for the Tube station.

14

I spent the next day with Sue, who showed me around the neighbourhood, and we caught a bus into the nearby town where I did some shopping, including a present for John and Sue.

On Saturday night, the evening of the party, John came to call for us.

'We thought we'd keep it local,' he said as he linked hands with Sue and we set off to walk down the road.

'Then we can all have a drink without worrying about driving,' Sue added.

'Good idea,' I replied as we entered.

I thought we'd left in plenty of time to arrive before the others, but there were several groups already in the bar, more were pouring in as we arrived, and the two were soon lost in a welter of greetings and chatter. All were couples, I thought wistfully. I seemed to be the only single person in the room.

'*Alex!* I wondered if you'd be here.'

My heartbeat quickened and I spun round at the sound of the familiar voice. 'Oh, Quinn! Hello!'

In trepidation I glanced over his shoulder for Caroline, but there was no sign of her. And in spite of all I had overheard that morning, I felt the muscles of my face break into a broad smile at the sight of his beloved figure.

And now, in this totally neutral setting, the realisation hit me like a punch in the stomach: that he *was* my beloved. No matter how hopeless and unrequited it was, no matter how much I suspected he might be on the make, no matter that I knew him to be a married man, it made not a jot of difference. I'd known for a long time how drawn I was to him, but this was different. This was the naked truth and something I would have to learn to live with.

But remembering the way we had parted, the way I'd shouted at him, made this meeting in public a rather awkward situation.

'Well,' I continued cautiously, 'Sue is one of my best friends. I'm surprised to see you though.'

Quinn looked steadily into my eyes. 'And John's one of mine! So of course I came along to wish them both well, and the timing was perfect — what with the exhibition.'

Of course. I should have remembered that he and John were such friends. I could have kicked myself. It should have been obvious that he would be here, especially as he'd said he was in London anyway. I was surprised Sue hadn't mentioned it, but of course she had so much else on her mind, it was understandable.

Apparently he was going to ignore the row, or had forgotten it, which was hard to believe. Whatever, it was all right by me.

'I decided to go and see it. The art exhibition, I mean.' I was still drinking in the sight and scent of him. His hair and beard had been neatly trimmed and he was wearing pale grey chinos and a blue long-sleeved, open-necked shirt patterned with grey swirls. I remembered the unknown woman's comment about him being an attractive man, and agreed wholeheartedly with her.

'What did you think of it?' Quinn took my elbow and steered me towards the bar. 'Let's get a drink, shall we?' I nodded.

'Very impressive,' I replied. 'They've certainly pulled out all the stops. Although it seemed a bit unreal actually, seeing my own painting in among so many others.'

'That's what I thought. It seemed smaller, somehow.' We'd reached the bar and Quinn was leaning an elbow on it as we waited to be served. All the seating was taken, so we'd propped ourselves against a windowsill in a corner and were sipping our drinks there.

'When are you going back?' Quinn shifted his position and put his glass on the sill.

'I thought Thursday. A few days to look around, do some shopping . . . '

'Well, that's a coincidence. So am I.' Our eyes met. 'Alex, would you like a lift back with me?' Quinn lifted an eyebrow. 'Quicker than the train, and you'd be company — stop me falling asleep at the wheel!'

'Oh! Well, er, I don't know.' I nibbled my lip as my thoughts raced. Would this lift include Caroline? If so, I'd rather walk than make up a third party. But . . . he had said . . . to keep him awake . . . So, perhaps not. 'I've got a return ticket.'

'Oh, never mind that, I'd really like you to.'

'Well, all right, that would be lovely. So, yes please,' I smiled. 'Much less hassle for me too.'

'Great. I'll pick you up on the way. After I've collected the painting. You've got my mobile number, haven't you?' I nodded.

I hadn't seen him approaching, but now realised that John had come quietly up behind us while we were talking and was beaming at us both. 'Hey, mate.' He thumped Quinn's shoulder. 'Glad you could make it. And Alex too, lovely to see you.'

'Wouldn't have missed it for the world.' Quinn grinned back. 'So you're actually going to tie the knot, then. I hope you and Sue will be really happy together.' He raised his glass. 'She's a great person.'

'Thanks, I can't argue with that. And I'm sure we will.' Then John's smile faded. 'No Caroline then? I thought she might have made the effort, just for old times' sake.'

Quinn briskly shook his head and took a step away, changing the subject. 'That looks a great buffet over there and I'm starving. Haven't eaten all day, been saving myself for tonight.' He laughed with what seemed like false heartiness. 'See you later, John,' he added as someone else came up to speak to his friend.

'Look, Alex,' he muttered, 'let's get another drink and a bite to eat and find

221

a quiet corner to sit down, if we can.'

We filled our plates and wandered out into the conservatory, which was deserted as everyone seemed to be crowding the bar area. Music started up and the din inside increased.

'We'll go back in a minute and be sociable. Right now I want a bit of peace and quiet.'

We settled ourselves in a couple of cane armchairs among some potted plants. Quinn stretched out his long legs and drew up a glass-topped table for our plates. He took a deep breath.

'I feel I need to apologise for the way I nagged at you over the phone. Looking back, I must have sounded a complete bully. But don't you think it's awkward talking on the phone when you can't see each other's faces?'

This was so exactly what I'd been thinking myself that I took a gulp of my drink too quickly and had to suppress a cough as it caught in my throat.

I nodded. 'Absolutely. And there's no need to apologise — you were only looking after my interests.'

I was still thinking about what John had said, and Quinn's reaction to it was intriguing me. So why not ask some questions? I thought. I had nothing to lose, after all.

'Quinn, what made you leave London and go back to Cornwall?' I asked casually. 'I'm not being nosy, but I overheard someone in the gallery mention your name, and how good you were at your job, and I just wondered . . .'

'Oh?' Quinn frowned as he turned in surprise. 'Who was that, then?'

'Just a couple in the crowd. I've no idea who they were.' I didn't elaborate, and a small silence fell between us.

Quinn looked into his drink and swirled it around, deep in his own thoughts. Then he drew in a deep breath and let it out in a sigh.

'Oh, heck, Alex.' Placing his drink back on the table, he looked up at me and spread his hands. 'It's a long story. But I suppose you might as well hear it from the beginning.' He gazed into the middle distance and tapped a finger on the tabletop.

'I believe I told you before, how I came up here as a student to do my training? When I qualified I was offered a very good post in that same gallery. It seemed too good to be true, and for a while it was.' He leaned back in his seat.

'It all went swimmingly at first. I was being paid a good salary, I had a full social life, a flat of my own and a wide circle of friends. I enjoyed what life had to offer and seized it with both hands.' His face darkened.

'Until I found I was getting more and more work pushed on me, for the same money, and the pressure built up. My superiors wanted a quicker turnover, and I couldn't make them understand that in my kind of work I had to be so careful and painstaking it couldn't *be* hurried. You know all about that.' He half-turned to me and I nodded, not wanting to interrupt now that he was at last opening up.

'So I told them if they wanted the job

done properly — and their reputation, of course, rested on it being done properly — they had to give me the time I needed. But nothing changed.'

He paused, temporarily lost in the past, head bent. 'Well, the mental pressure became so bad, on top of the grief . . . I mean, the personal problems I was having as well, that eventually I had a total breakdown.'

So it had been true, then, what the woman had said. I glanced down at that curly head and had to forcibly restrain myself from laying a sympathetic hand on it.

But, grief? I frowned, but he was talking and I didn't want to interrupt.

'I spent weeks, months, in rehab.' Quinn glanced at me and our eyes held. 'It gave me plenty of time to think things over, until at last I gained some sort of control over my life again. And after a while I decided that my former existence was no longer right for me. The stress that went with the job just wasn't worth my mental health.' He paused, picked up his drink and took a sip.

'So I tossed it all overboard and came back to Cornwall to set up on my own. That was five years ago, and it was the best thing I've ever done. I was still only twenty-six then, although I felt like an old man.' He straightened up and his face cleared.

So he's only two years older than me, I thought. As if it mattered. What I still didn't know, however, was where and when he had married his Caroline, and where she came into the story. But Quinn had started speaking again, so maybe now . . .

'I wasn't hard up,' he went on, 'it was so much cheaper to live down there, and I'd been earning good money in London, so I had savings. I started on the wood carving, which was something I'd always wanted to do and had never found time or opportunity for.' He smiled. 'As a boy I was always whittling bits of wood. Now I could do it seriously.'

He smiled. 'Alex, it was the best therapy I could have wished for. I set up the art business to bring in the daily bread and butter, and after a shaky start, it's just about holding its own now. The carvings are becoming popular too.'

He paused and our eyes met. 'And when I look out of the window, at the beauty around me down there in St. Ives — ' He jerked a thumb. ' — and compare it with where I lived in the city, I breathe a sigh of relief that I got out when I did.'

'I know. I thought the same the other day. City life is like being on another planet compared with Cornwall.'

A silence fell after Quinn's voice faltered and died, and the sounds of the party drifted over our heads as I waited for more.

The silence lengthened as I waited. Was that it? It seemed to be. All he was prepared to tell me, anyway.

'I see,' I said at last. 'Thanks for telling me all that, Quinn.' Our eyes met for a moment. 'I'm so glad you came through it all and made the right decision. But it must have been a wrench. It took courage to throw it all up and make a totally new lifestyle for yourself. Do you never have any regrets?'

Quinn shrugged. 'Sometimes, if I'm honest, I miss the challenge of the work I used to do. That's why I was so keen to have a go at the Nicholson — and so pleased, after all my doubts, to find I hadn't lost my touch.'

'Well, maybe when people see that one in the exhibition, perhaps they'll search you out with commissions, even in deepest Cornwall!'

Quinn chuckled and the mood lightened. 'Only in my dreams, I guess. And I don't really think I want them to. I'm very happy as I am.' He lifted the last of a sausage roll to his mouth and, brushing off crumbs, rose to his feet.

'Do you think we ought to go and join the others?' he said, the smile still on his face. 'I think they're about to have a toast to Sue and John.'

'Yes, of course. We *are* being a bit unsociable.'

'There'll be more time to talk in the car.' Quinn pulled out my chair for me as I picked up my glass and joined him.

15

I met Quinn as arranged, and we started out on the long drive back to Cornwall, with the painting stowed away in the boot along with our bags. I was looking forward to spending the time during the journey on trying to get him to open up about himself again.

The roads were busy, but there were no actual hold-ups, and we made good time, arriving at the Exeter service station for lunch as we had hoped. As it happened, there was no opportunity for personal chat; Quinn was concentrating on the traffic, and the constant noise of it made conversation difficult. Apart from the radio and various remarks of little importance between us, it had been a disappointing journey so far in terms of conversation.

The restaurant was full of families, and the clatter of cutlery and buzz of chattering crowds again drowned out anything other than trivia. Some small children were running around, bored with waiting for their meal, and when I glanced up from my salad I noticed Quinn watching them intently, with an expression on his face I couldn't quite identify. Then, when a little girl of perhaps two or three years old tripped and fell, right beside our table, he immediately pushed back his chair and jumped up. Tenderly lifting the child to her feet with a comforting murmur, he held her hand until the mother came hurrying across to collect her.

'You're fond of children, Quinn, are you?' I said as he returned to his seat.

He flinched as I spoke and to my surprise I noticed his face had paled. 'Well, er, the fact is, Alex ... ' he mumbled, then pushed his half-eaten pasta to one side with a gesture of impatience. 'Oh, hang it all, you might as well know. The fact is, I've only told you part of it. I suppose I should have told you the rest, but it still hurts to think about it, even after all this time.'

I felt my eyes widen and drew in a quick breath as I noticed the raw pain on his face.

'Quinn, only tell me if you feel up to it,' I said with sympathy, although I was itching to know what memories were affecting him so badly.

'Let's get out of here, grab a coffee and sit on a bench outside where it's quieter.' He strode towards the coffee machine, picked up the two cardboard cups and we left.

There was a free bench on a grassy mound under a tree and we made a beeline for it. It was a pleasantly warm day and quite comfortable there in the sun, although a few leftover summer flowers were beginning to wilt in tubs nearby, and the leaves of the plane tree above us had just started turning.

Quinn bent down and placed his coffee on the concrete surround of the seat to cool, then leant forward and rested his forearms on his knees.

'Alex, I've never told you about my

marriage, have I?' A jolt swept through me and I only just managed not to splutter into my cup.

'No, but I gathered from things John has said, that you are. Married, I mean.'

'Oh?' Quinn turned to me and frowned. 'Then you must know, too, that Caroline and I are separated.'

Stars exploded behind my eyes. '*Separated?* No, I didn't.' I felt the corners of my mouth lift and stifled the flicker of pleasure that was threatening to betray me. For this explained so much. The tender looks and gestures, the warm hugs, that almost-kiss . . . But 'separated' could mean they were still legally married, of course. In which case, nothing had changed. My smile faded.

Quinn sighed and bent down to pick up his drink. Taking a long pull, he nursed it in his hands and looked down into it as he swirled the liquid around.

'As for the reason why . . . You mentioned children.' He paused. 'We had a child once, a little girl. She died,' he said abruptly, raising haunted eyes to my face.

I gasped. This was so unexpected.

'Oh, Quinn, I'm so sorry.' I reached for his hand and gently squeezed it. 'That's terribly inadequate, but I don't know what else to say.' He returned the pressure with a grip that made my knuckles crack, and swallowed hard.

'She would have been a bit older now than that kid in there.' He jerked his head towards the restaurant. 'Blonde and blue-eyed, just like her.' His gaze had shifted to somewhere far away as his voice cracked, then paused.

A silence fell while I let him recover. Then, tentatively, I asked softly, 'How . . . what happened . . . to cause . . . was it an illness?'

He shook his head slowly. 'No. She fell from a tree in the park and landed on the concrete path. She caught her head on the edge of the kerb.'

Quinn rubbed a hand across his forehead. 'It was instantaneous. There was nothing anyone could do. She was only up on the first branch, and I'd been holding her hand until then. But Caroline spoke to me and I turned . . . it was only a split-second . . . that was all it took.' There were tears openly standing in his eyes now. He dashed them roughly away with the back of a hand.

I felt a lump rising to my own throat and swallowed.

'As time went on, it felt as if we were living in a void. The place seemed so *empty*, Alex.' Our eyes met and held.

'Then Caroline and I started having rows. I knew deep down she blamed me for the accident, although she never said so outright, nor even hinted. And I suppose I subconsciously blamed *her*. For distracting me.' Quinn shrugged and his shoulders sagged. He looked grey and haggard.

'Eventually, it all became too much, and we broke up. That was four years ago, and now we're divorcing. That was the other reason I came to London, to see Caroline and sign some papers.'

I let all my breath out in a long sigh. For this explained so much. Quinn's reticence, his reserve, and the feeling I'd always had that there was something more, some secret he kept close to himself. Why I had felt some kind of invisible barrier between us.

Then, as what he had just said sank in, in spite of all my concern and sympathy for what he had been through, a little flutter of hope had begun to unfurl inside me. Like the tender shoot of some delicate plant, it was slowly making its way up towards the light.

'But we'd better be on our way.' Quinn glanced at his watch. 'We should have been on the road before this. I hadn't realised how much time I'd wasted.'

'Quinn, it wasn't wasted.' I laid a hand on his arm. 'Thank you for telling me, and I'm more sorry than I can ever say.'

Sorry for him, of course, and for Caroline. But for me? The future had in such a short time taken on a whole new aspect that, although I chided myself for being selfish, I couldn't help but indulge in some pleasant daydreams as we sped homewards.

★　★　★

We were nearing Hayle, almost at the end of our journey, when it happened and I was instantly shaken out of my reverie.

I had been vaguely aware of the huge, high-sided delivery lorry that had been following us for some time, as long as a small house. I'd marvelled how that a thing that size could negotiate Cornish roads.

'That chap's itching to overtake us,' I remarked as the vehicle drew nearer. 'He's been edging closer for ages, waiting for a chance.'

'Silly fool,' Quinn replied, glancing in the mirror. 'Far too risky. The road's much too narrow and there's a sharp bend up ahead.'

'He's going to, though — oh, Quinn, watch out!' I gripped the shelf in front of me as the vehicle loomed closer.

But, due to its high sides, the driver must have misjudged the distance between us. Or not seen our car at all. Suddenly Quinn swore under his breath, braked and pulled over. But it was too late. The lorry clipped our wing and we were hurled off the road and into the undergrowth. I saw a hedge looming up in front, the sun glinting off steel railings at the top. I heard a scream — my own. And Quinn's shout. Then everything went black as I passed out.

* * *

When I came round and opened my eyes I found I was lying on the grass verge. Somewhere high above me, lost in the patch of blue sky, a lark was pouring its heart out in joyous song. To my right a fat bumblebee was working a stand of red clover and a small determined insect was crawling up a stem of waving grass. Nature going about its business, unconcerned with the troubles of mere mortals.

I raised my head. A paramedic was kneeling beside me, feeling my feet and legs. That's in case I've broken anything, I thought woozily.

'Hi there, miss. How are you feeling now you've come back to us?'

'All right I think,' I replied cautiously. 'M . . . my head's going round a bit, and I feel sick, but that's all.'

'You're going to be OK,' the man said cheerily. 'There's no major damage. Can you manage to sit up if I help you?' I nodded, which was not the best thing to do as it made me more dizzy than ever.

'Yes, I think so,' I replied as he put an arm around my shoulders.

My head was clearing now I was upright although I still felt queasy. That's the shock, I told myself wisely. It'll pass. I took a long swig from the water he was offering me and felt much better.

'You were just knocked out, my handsome.' The broad Cornish voice was very comforting. 'Apart from a few cuts and bruises, you'll be fine,' he added with a reassuring smile.

Then as the last few bits of cloud in my head cleared away, I remembered everything. Urgently I clutched at his arm. 'Quinn!' I looked up at him in consternation. 'My friend . . . How . . . What . . . Is *he* all right?'

'Don't you worry now. He's OK. A bit shaken up, like you, with bruises that put yours in the shade, but nothing serious. He's over there, behind the car.' He jerked his head. 'My mate's given him a thorough going-over. I don't think either of you need hospital treatment. You were very lucky indeed.'

Breathing a sigh of relief at this news, I struggled to my feet.

'And the lorry driver?'

'Gone to hospital. A few broken bones. He'll live,' my rescuer replied. 'Now, are you sure you're OK?'

'Yes, yes, I am. I'm fine,' I said,

looking down my left leg at the ripped jeans and the enormous bruise that was showing through the gap. The medic had put something soothing on it and on my painful elbow as well.

'Thanks so much for your help.' I managed a shaky smile.

'Well, if you're sure, I'll get back to the van and put all this stuff away.'

Only then did I notice the emergency equipment laid out on the verge. And the police cars. And the 'road closed' sign. The overturned lorry blocking both carriageways.

And our car halfway up the hedge, with the driver's door stove in. It had stopped just clear of those wicked-looking railings. I drew in a long breath. We had been so lucky. Shakily picking my way through the chaos, I went to look for Quinn.

He'd been coming to find me too, and we met just as I was skirting the lorry. Laughing and crying at the same time, I flew into his arms and then he was hugging me as if he'd never let me go. I wrapped my arms around his waist and buried my head in his chest. We stayed like that for a long moment, locked in an embrace which at that time had nothing romantic about it. We were just two people clinging together to express our relief, our thanks that we were still alive, and the pure physical comfort that such closeness to another person can give.

'Oh, Alex! Are you all right? They told me you were, but I had to see for myself before I believed it.' Quinn held me at arm's length and looked me critically up and down.

I nodded. 'Perfectly. How about you?' I returned the scrutiny. He had a black eye and a long, raw scratch down one cheek, but that was all I could see.

'I twisted my knee as we went sideways, but they say that will heal on its own. Apart from that and what you see,' he indicated his face, 'I'm OK.'

'Oh, we were so lucky. When I felt the car leave the road, I thought . . . '

'I know. So did I.'

'So what happens next? How are we going to get home now?'

'Where do you two live?' came a voice from behind me. I whirled around to see a tall police officer smiling down at us.

'St. Ives,' Quinn and I said together.

'Ah, right. Just wait there a minute. I'll be back.' The man turned and strode off.

'Do you think he's going to help us?' I raised an eyebrow at Quinn, who shrugged.

'Seems like it.'

The policeman was soon back with another, shorter man at his side.

'You're in luck,' he said. 'This is Jim, my brother. He's come up from St. Ives to pick up his kids from school. He was held up by the accident and got out when he saw me. He's going back now we've got the diversion in place. He'll give you a lift.'

'Oh, wonderful!' I turned to Jim with a broad smile. Quinn stepped forward and extended a hand.

'That's really good of you,' he said as they shook hands. 'I'm Quinn and this is Alex.'

'A pleasure,' he replied. 'There's plenty of room for three in the back. I'll go and tell the children to squeeze up a bit. You'd better get your stuff out of the car and bring it over. Mine's the black Toyota over there. I'll go and organise some space.'

Quinn and I crossed to the car, which had been removed from the bank by the heavy-duty breakdown truck that was now working on the lorry.

'They phoned the AA just now,' Quinn remarked. 'Someone'll be here soon to tow her home for me.' He laid a hand on the door of the boot and surveyed the damage to the wing. 'Poor old car,' he said ruefully. 'I doubt she'll ever be the same again.'

'But Quinn, think . . . it could have been a complete write-off.' He nodded and opened the boot.

All our belongings were in a mangled mess, jumbled up together where they had been thrown by the impact. And the painting was lying underneath them all.

'Oh! I hope that's all right.' I drew in a breath as Quinn lifted the suitcases out, and I gently drew the picture towards me.

Then my heart lurched as one corner of it moved under my hand. 'Quinn, feel this! Tell me it's not what I think.' I stood aside while he slowly felt all round the edges of it. Then his smile faded as our eyes met and we both knew.

'It's broken.'

And all the way home, while forcing myself to make polite conversation with Jim's teenage sons, I was wondering and worrying about what we might find when we eventually unwrapped my precious painting.

16

'Where would you like me to drop you?' Jim's voice brought me back to earth and I realised we were entering St. Ives. The familiar scent of salt air, seaweed and the faint tang of fish was wafting in through the window and I would have known with my eyes shut that we were home.

'Oh, I think my place, don't you, Quinn? It won't take Jim so far out of his way.'

'Sure. That's the next right, OK?'

After making our farewells and thanks, I felt in my bag for the key and we carried everything inside the cottage.

'I must look at this before we do anything else, even put the kettle on,' I said, lifting the painting on to the table. I drew it out of my laptop case and carefully began to unwrap it.

Quinn hovered at my shoulder as, hardly daring to breath, I drew it out. Then we both gasped. One corner of the frame had completely snapped through and was hanging loose, while the painting had two long gouges up one side.

'Oh my god! Look at that! As he spoke, Quinn's face drained of colour and I felt physically sick.

'It's ruined,' I said flatly and turned to bury my face in his shoulder. He put one arm around me and patted me absently on the back as hot tears pricked my eyelids. 'After all your work . . . after . . . everything . . . ' I finished lamely. I sank into a chair and put my head in my hands.

Quinn was lifting the painting to peer more closely at it. 'Alex, I think I might be able to do something to it. Put it in a new frame, certainly, so it won't be as bad as it looks. And I might be able to touch up those scratches, although they'll always be visible.'

'*Could* you?' I shot upright. 'Oh,

Quinn, that would be absolutely wonderful.'

Quinn gave me a long, serious look. 'You do realise it will have completely lost its value now, don't you? I'm afraid the damage makes it next to worthless on the market.'

I stood and slipped an arm through his. 'Can you believe,' I said slowly, 'that deep down inside, I don't really mind about that?'

'What do you mean, you don't mind! You owned a picture worth thousands and you don't care that you've lost it?' He stared at me in amazement.

'You may think I'm mad,' I replied, 'but if it were worth all that money I'd be scared to display it in case it got stolen or damaged. I'd have to keep it in a bank vault, and what good would that be? Hidden away where nobody could see it.'

I turned on a heel and spread my hands. 'Great art should be seen and appreciated. Be *enjoyed*.'

And, inwardly, there was another

reason why I was not brokenhearted over the way things had turned out. I'd lost a fortune, yes, but I had enough with the cottage and the legacy to live a comfortable life. And it would prove once and for all how misguided I'd been to have ever doubted Quinn's motives and integrity.

'And when I think, Quinn, how we could have been killed in that accident . . . It puts it all in perspective somehow. Do you see what I mean?'

He sank down onto the window seat and folded his arms, holding himself as if he felt cold. Slowly he nodded.

'Alex, you're absolutely right. It makes me shiver to think about it.'

I joined him on the long seat and he looked at me with his soul in his eyes. Then he reached for my hand and my fingers closed around his.

'Because,' he said slowly, 'although I wasn't going to say all this yet . . . if I ever lost you, I wouldn't want to carry on living.'

My heart lurched and a lightning bolt

of awareness shot through me.

'Alex, my darling, you must know how much I love you. Have done since that first day you came into the shop, and you were covered in embarrassment after you'd fallen into my lap on the train. And to save your blushes, and mine, I pretended not to remember.'

He smiled a slow steady smile that melted my heart, as I gazed back at him. This was something that had haunted my dreams for so long it had taken on the guise of a fairytale.

'Because I found I was falling in love with you.'

What? The voice was not much more than a murmur, but I felt my jaw drop. This was a fairytale no longer. Then the walls suddenly seemed to sway as it sank in. Love me? Quinn loved *me*! I stared at him in disbelief, my head whirling.

'But I've been holding back because I didn't know how you felt about me.'

'Oh, Quinn!' My voice cracked. 'I've loved you too. From that first time in the studio as well. But when John said about your marriage — in the pub that night, do you remember? I thought it was hopeless.'

Quinn's arms were round me now and my head rested on his shoulder. I felt as if I had come home at last. To where I truly belonged.

Quinn sighed. 'And I had no idea. Oh, Alex, my darling, what a lot of time it's taken for us to understand each other!' He put a finger under my chin and tilted my face up to his.

'But you've never talked about your marriage . . . You still wear a ring.' He touched my wedding band with his thumb. 'Yes, I know it's on the other hand, but it's still a constant reminder, and I didn't know . . . ' His voice tailed off.

'Oh, Quinn, I'd have told you if you'd asked.' I slowly shook my head. 'But I didn't think . . . didn't know you cared. But I'll tell you now.' I sat up and took both his hands in mine. 'My marriage was so painful I've never told anyone the whole of it.' I looked down at the ring and impatiently snatched it off. I realised I'd subconsciously gone on wearing it as a warning against ever getting involved with a man again. But now . . . ?

'Paul and I have been separated now for over two years. I'm about to file for divorce.' I pushed the ring into the deepest corner of my pocket. 'It was the biggest mistake I ever made, but I was completely taken in by him. He was a charmer, but a lazy, selfish, and unfaithful charmer.' My voice caught on a sob. 'Nobody knew . . . nobody realised. Other people thought it was a marriage made in heaven.' I felt a tear sliding down my cheek. Quinn reached out a finger and tenderly wiped it away.

'So is it any wonder I vowed never to get into another relationship? I kept myself from showing my feelings, even when I was being drawn towards you. In case I was let down again. I just couldn't stand going through all that a second time, you see.'

I saw the immense sympathy on Quinn's face now as he absorbed my story. At last he gave a deep sigh and relaxed into the seat.

'I'm truly sorry about all that,' he said at last. His gaze was still fixed on my face.

A silence fell. A throbbing silence as our eyes held. Then we both reached out at the same time and fell into each other's arms. Like one in a dream I felt him lay his cheek against my hair, then put a warm finger under my chin and tilt my face up to his again.

Dreamlike, I felt his mouth come down to mine, soft, gentle, then becoming more urgent until I found myself rising to meet him, my hands winding themselves of their own accord more closely round his neck. It had been a long time since I'd been held like this and my body, responding to an inner need, pressed itself against him.

'So you see,' I whispered against his cheek, gently stroking the broken skin, 'that's the reason why I couldn't tell you what I really felt. Like you, I was afraid of being let down again. But, oh Quinn, I've loved you so much, all through these weeks, months . . . the strain when we've been together so much and at the same time so apart.'

I was in a daze, marvelling over how all our doubts had, in such a short space of time, turned into this glorious, wonderful, unimaginable dream! My heart was singing, and I knew a smile like sunlight was spreading across my face.

It was more than I could take in. Words were beyond me, although I heard myself murmuring little crooning noises into his neck. There was a tiny pulse throbbing there; I could feel it steadily beating under my cheek. Quinn's breath was warm against my hair as slowly, unhurriedly, I gave myself up to the feel of his lean body against mine, breathed in the clean, fresh smell of him, and relaxed totally.

In the momentary quietness that had fallen, I could hear the scream of seagulls overhead and the wash of waves in the harbour. I became aware of the sun streaming through the window, and the patch of blue sky. Outwardly nothing had changed, but as my spirits soared, suddenly I noticed what a lovely day it was.

'So, how about putting that kettle on now?' Quinn said as we surfaced at last, and both laughed aloud in our newly-found togetherness.

Reluctantly I unwound myself from his arms and began to become aware of normal life passing by outside. The laughter of happy children, the stir and bustle of a town going about its business. Unaware of the momentous events that had been taking place in our lives.

Then we just talked and talked, discovering all there was left to know about each other.

So much had happened in this last momentous couple of days. More than I had ever dreamt. Maybe the accident itself had been a catalyst for this wonderful new closeness between us, for if I'd caught the train none of it would have happened.

And as we talked, all the pain and strain of my former life, and any doubts I'd ever had about Quinn, faded away like mist before the sun, until there was nothing left but the two of us.

★ ★ ★

'Alex,' said Quinn some time later as we relaxed over a meal, 'you told me once that you were never going to sell the painting, or hang it on the wall here. What *were* you thinking of doing with it?'

'I've always wanted to give it to the Penlee gallery to hang with all the others of the Newlyn painters. It's where I feel it belongs. And I think Granny Lou would approve of that. Don't you?'

Quinn nodded slowly nodded, then a broad smile spread across his face. 'That would be utterly perfect,' he murmured. 'Maybe we could even take her there to see it, one day. And Alex,' he added, 'remember, she knew even before we did ourselves, that we were meant for each other. She's a wise old lady, isn't she?'

I nodded happily. Oh, what a summer this had been! Not only had I solved the riddle of the painting and discovered a little family history, but I'd found the love of my life as well. And there would never be any secrets between us again.